MA-AH, MA-AH, MURDER!

A TAMSIN KERNICK ENGLISH COZY MYSTERY

BOOK 5

LUCY EMBLEM

CHAPTER ONE

"There you go, Quizzy darling, we'll have your paw better in no time."

Tamsin gave her biggest dog a hug as Quiz happily munched the butter-covered pill she'd been given, even happier that Tamsin was shovelling in more treats to make sure the pill was well and truly swallowed.

"How's her paw doing?" asked Emerald with concern in her voice.

"It was a nasty cut alright - fancy leaving broken glass in the grass!"

"Awful. People can be so thoughtless ... I suppose that's one of the hazards of summer - people having picnics and leaving their rubbish behind."

Tamsin straightened up. "But the vet says it should heal well with these antibiotics. I'm taking her in to get the dressing changed tomorrow - they need to check the stitches have held. Paws can be so difficult."

"Hard to explain to her that she can't run about with the others."

"It is. Shame with this amazing weather we're having. They love the stream when it's this hot. I've offered her some good books, but she just doesn't seem interested," Tamsin grinned and ruffled Quiz's head as she lay on her dog-bed, her chin resting on her bandaged paw, a picture of boredom. "But she's very patient. We'll go for great walks again when you're better, poppet," and she bent over and planted a kiss on the top of

Quiz's head. Banjo and Moonbeam came over to see if they could get buttery pills too, but had to make do with a little biscuit each and a snuggle.

"Do you think the antibiotics will affect her? Apart from keeping the wound clean, I mean!"

"They do say they kill off all the good bacteria too. I know Muffin had tummy trouble after Charity had to give her antibiotics last year."

"How about giving her some live yogurt, to put the bacteria back again?" Emerald tossed her long blonde plait back over her shoulder.

"That's a great idea! Why didn't I think of that? I'll have to go and get some."

"Tell you what - I'm going over to Susannah's today, you know - that crazy goatkeeper? I want to get some more of her lovely goat soap. You can get some real goat's yogurt - even better! *And* it'll save me cycling and getting boiled."

Tamsin laughed, "The first time you told me you used goat soap on your face I could hardly believe it!"

"It's lovely!" Emerald pouted. "And because it's handmade, and Susannah's so fussy about what she puts in her products, I know it's ok for my skin. I've got a few of my yoga students buying from her now. And she's making cheese as well."

"Isn't goats' cheese smelly?'

"Depends what sort you have. I've tried some nice hard cheese she does. Works out a bit too expensive for every day. Hey, you had some last week on that mushroom pasta I made, don't you remember?"

"Ohh, I had no idea that was goats' cheese! I guess that answers my question. Yeah, let's go up to Susannah's for a forage. She's open today? On a Sunday?"

"She's always open. She does the Farmers' Market in Malvern some Saturdays. I guess the goats have to be milked every day anyway."

"Of course. Farming is hard work. Wouldn't catch me doing it - especially in this heat!"

"Let's go now, before it gets any hotter."

As they ascended the Malvern Hills in Tamsin's trusty Top Dogs van,

Emerald pointed out the hawks lazily circling on the thermals beside the hills.

"I always find it amazing that when I'm up on the Beacon I can look down and see the hawks hovering and squealing below me," said Tamsin with a smile. She loved these Hills!

As they descended the Hills again, they could see sheep lying cudding in the shade of the huge clumps of gorse. Susannah's small-holding was right round the other side of the Malverns, on a back road between Colwall and Wellington Heath. They could see the goats in the front pasture as they turned up the bumpy drive to the farmstead.

"Aren't they gorgeous!" exclaimed Emerald, clinging to the door handle as the van lurched from pothole to pothole.

"They're such a lovely clean bright white - hang on, got to keep my eyes on the road .."

"There's a dip coming - I usually get off the bike there and push."

"I'm guessing that goat-farming doesn't pay well."

"I think Susannah's like us - oof!" The slender Emerald bounced up in the air and back onto the seat, "that was a big one! Driven to do what she loves. As long as she can make ends meet I guess she's happy."

"I'm quite sure she'd be happier if she got paid for her pains .. I find it helps to make up for the difficult dog training clients when I know I'm getting more than the minimum wage."

They at last reached the top of the lane, parked next to a ramshackle red - faded to pink - goat trailer, and stepped out into the sunshine to admire the view. Some of the goats bleated hopefully and ambled up to the fence to see if there were any goodies on offer.

"Sorry goats, I've got nothing for you. I wouldn't know what to give you anyway," said Tamsin, automatically feeling in her pockets. "I guess dog kibble and dried sprats is not a good idea."

Emerald was reaching over the fence and scratching the head of one of the friendlier goats. "They're very curious," she said.

"And what amazing eyes they have! They look super-intelligent."

"Oh, they are!" They turned at the voice and saw Susannah heading towards them. "Can you see the fixings on the stable doors over there? The bolts have to be tilted down so they can't open them."

"Hi Susannah!" said Emerald. "How do they reach them?"

"Those beautiful long necks let them lean right over. You can see the cross-bars on the doors are on the outside too, so they can't stand on them."

"Know your enemy!" laughed Tamsin, coming forward to introduce herself. "Essential to animal management. I know just what my dogs are capable of, so I can pre-empt problems."

"You've got it!" smiled Susannah. "You have to know their escape-ability! I have a few lively British Alpines and Toggenburgs - they're those black and white and hairy brown ones over by the hedge - and they sure can jump! The bulk of the herd is the quieter British Saanens you see, the white ones. I sometimes have to keep the coloured goatlings in a pen where I've added a lid so they can't jump out!"

"*Goatlings?* Is that for real? Or is that your nickname for them?" asked Emerald, enchanted.

"Oh yes, it's real! A goatling is one who hasn't yet kidded - teenage hooligans, the lot of them," she smiled lovingly at the curious goats still gathered at the gate, waiting for something to happen. "So you're Tamsin - I've heard you do great things at your dog school. Charity keeps me up to speed with the news."

"Ah, of course! Charity knows everyone," nodded Tamsin.

"And you do it all without being nasty to the dogs, I hear."

"S'right. Can't bear animal cruelty." Tamsin reached to touch the face of the goat that was nuzzling her.

"Me too. These goats mean so much to me. They're all my own breeding - one big family. I can remember when you were born, Lilac," she said to the goat Tamsin was stroking. "And you see Marigold over there? She's the grandma of many of them."

"Do they all have flower names?" asked Emerald, entranced.

"Flowers, herbs, spices, all natural things. There's Nutmeg the brown Togg nibbling the hedge! Parsley is the one with the floppy ear, Dahlia and her kid Pansy are just over there ..."

"They look beautifully clean and content," said Emerald, who'd gone back to scratching offered heads.

"And look at those full bellies!" said Tamsin.

"They spend all day eating and cudding, making lots of lovely milk for me."

"Do they sleep out here at night?"

"Oh, goodness no! Well, not usually. Only in very hot, dry weather would they condescend to sleeping outside. So I'll see if any of them want to stay out tonight - this heatwave is something else!" she said, fanning her face with her hand. "They love their comfort, and they absolutely *hate* rain. One raindrop results in pandemonium as they all race for the field shelter! Want to see where they live? I've just finished mucking out." And she led them over to the stable block. It was made up of three very large loose boxes - one for kids and goatlings, one for goats with very young kids at foot, and one for everyone else. There were also smaller pens for goats who needed to be separate - for kidding, Susannah explained, or on the rare occasions they were sick or injured. Round the other side of the block was another smaller building, for her two males.

"You keep them away from the females?" asked Tamsin.

"Can you not smell them!" laughed Susannah as they walked over towards the block. Tamsin wrinkled her nose while Emerald put her hand over hers. "They have to be in a separate place or they'd taint the milk. I even have a different stock-coat to wear when I'm handling them. That's where the idea of goats being smelly comes from - the billies really *are* smelly!"

"But the females aren't!" said Emerald, smelling her hands which she'd stroked the goats with.

"No, they smell gorgeous - of fresh hay and warmth. But when they come on heat they find the smell of the billies quite irresistible!"

"You love them." Tamsin stated, looking admiringly at Susannah.

"I do. Otherwise I wouldn't be working my fingers to the bone, day in, day out, summer and winter, Christmas Day and all. Come and see the kids - I was just going to give them their bottles. Want to have a go?"

Tamsin and Emerald looked like schoolkids offered a big treat, "Oh yes please!" they chorussed.

And they spent a happy few minutes being shown how to hold the bottles, and how tightly to hang on to them as the kids' powerful jaws suckled them. They laughed to see the expression in the little kids' eyes turn from ravenously hungry to sated and sleepy, as they made little coughs to clear the last milky drips from their throats.

"We arrived at just the right time," said Tamsin, carrying her two bottles as they crossed the yard to the dairy block.

"Here, I'll wash and sterilise those in a minute," said Susannah, taking an armful of bottles into one of the rooms and leaving them in the sink. "Tell me what you're after today. Your usual soap, Emerald?"

"Yes please - I'd like to try your mint soap today, as well as the honey one."

"And I'd like some yogurt please. I have a dog on antibiotics and I'm told it'll help her recover."

"Oh definitely - nothing better! And goats' milk is so easy on the stomach too."

"She's not ill," Tamsin added quickly - proud of the health of her dogs, "she has a badly-gashed paw."

And so they made their purchases. "You must spend half your life cleaning," said Emerald, gazing at the gleaming stainless steel buckets and vats and shelving everywhere, and the wet floor.

"I do. Have to pass all sorts of tests regularly. Do you know, when the inspector first came out he sat in the kitchen in the house over there, drinking my tea, and saying that raw goats' milk would never pass the tests as it tasted so awful. I said 'Would you like some more tea?' 'Yes please,' he answers, 'very nice, thank you.' 'So you're enjoying the goats' milk?' I says, staring him in the face."

"What did he do?" Tamsin's mouth was open, waiting for the answer.

"He looked flustered and actually blushed as I poured the milk into his cup! And I'm proud to say that my milk has never failed a test, ever."

"He can put that in his pipe and smoke it!" laughed Tamsin. "Thank goodness I don't have to pass tests. The halls I use have to pass health and safety, and fire regulations and all that, of course."

"You're always studying though, aren't you," Emerald put in, "And you've got all those letters after your name. You kind of test yourself!"

"True. But I think we all have the same aims - to do our very best for our customers. And for me and Susannah, that means being a slave to our animals."

Susannah smiled and gazed out at her herd of contented goats. Most were now lying down cudding in the sunshine, eyes half-closed. "When I first started out I had a shepherd who would help me with any difficult kiddings. He was great. I learned such a lot from him." She turned back to them with a bright smile, "Paddy used to say this wasn't a goat farm, it was a goat hotel!"

"So it should be!" smiled Tamsin in return, warming to Susannah by the minute. "People tell me I'm too soft with my dogs, but I try to get softer all the time. And I can tell you that Emerald's Opal is the most pampered cat in Worcestershire!"

And so they took their purchases and started on the bumpy journey off the farmstead.

"What a lovely person!" Tamsin said to Emerald as they reached the smooth road again. "I don't know how I've missed meeting her up to now."

"Too many Saturday training sessions," said Emerald. "Perhaps you should take a break sometimes."

"And you know that practically never happens," smiled Tamsin, as they headed home.

CHAPTER TWO

Quiz's paw healed nicely. And she was right as rain and flying about with the other dogs in what seemed like no time at all. She enjoyed her yogurt, and Tamsin started to give it to all the dogs regularly, as well as enjoying it herself on her breakfast oats. With the weather still being so unusually hot, she was actually tearing herself from her bed earlier than usual and walking the dogs before the heat of the day. They enjoyed the coolness of the stream, and while they frolicked in the water, Tamsin relished the tiny wild strawberries that grew in a secret place amongst the brambles. She actually got to meet a whole new set of dog-walkers on these morning forays - those who walked their dogs before going to work every day.

As ever, folk admired how well-behaved her dogs were, and complained that their own dog was too slow, or too stupid, or too stubborn, to come when called. And as ever, Tamsin forebore to tell them that it was they who were too slow, too stupid, or too stubborn to learn how to teach their dog, and just signed them up for class instead!

After one of these early walks she came back to find Emerald brandishing the coffee pot. "Just finished my yoga practice. Want a coffee?"

"Is the Pope a Catholic?" smiled Tamsin as she re-filled the dogs' water bucket, and sent them to find some shade in the garden where their coats could dry without making their beds damp.

Emerald clattered the coffee things and, being in a chirpy mood, said, "Know who I bumped into yesterday in town?"

"Who?" said Tamsin through a mouthful of the apple she was slicing into her breakfast bowl.

"Linda!"

"Ah, Andrew's landlady. And how's she getting on with the Health shop? I haven't been in there for a while. All good?"

"She says she's loving it and wonders why she didn't think of something like this before."

"Probably because there already was a health shop in Malvern ..."

"I suppose so. Anyhow, she's formed the most unlikely friendship with Rosie!"

"Ah Rosie - the, shall we say, rather rough kid who worked in the shop under the previous management? Linda knocking off some of the sharp edges?"

"Apparently she's becoming a model of customer service."

"Amazing. But that's good. She certainly seems to be a worker. And quite an oddball, as I remember."

"She's definitely one of a kind. So that's all working out well," she plonked a steaming mug down in front of Tamsin. "But she said something odd happened."

"Oh yes?" Tamsin felt her ears prick, like her little terrier Moonbeam's, and she stopped chewing.

"Yeah. She gets the scones and buns for her little café area from a lady in Upton-upon-Severn. She only needs a few and the Furies are fully booked - that's why she doesn't have the same cakes as Jean-Philippe."

Jean-Philippe at The Cake Stop, the best coffee shop in town, got all his exotic and lavish cakes from Dodds & Co, known locally as The Three Furies because of their ancient Greek names and indomitable characters, while Linda provided tea and plainer fare for her customers in the health shop.

"Anyhow," she sat down opposite Tamsin at their little table, "she had to send a batch of scones back last week. They looked as good as usual, but customers were complaining that they tasted funny."

"That's bad."

"Rosie tried one and pulled an awful face, apparently!"

"That's my Rosie!"

"Well the supplier's a nice lady - Hilda. You may have seen her at the Farmers' Market - she does plain bakes, like fruit cake, scones, biscuits .."

"Oh yeah, I've had one of her peanut biscuits - scrumptious! So what's with the scones tasting funny? That doesn't sound like her."

"Exactly. She was mortified and delivered a new batch to Linda the very next day, refusing any money for them. She's really upset, understandably. Worried she'll get thrown out of the Market, for a start."

"So what was wrong with them? Bad buttermilk? Rotten eggs?"

"This is what's puzzling her, according to Linda. Everything she used was just the same as usual. Hilda's convinced someone interfered with her scones for some mad reason."

"That's awful! You mean like those weird people who put glass in baby foods and caused all the manufacturers to make their packaging tamperproof. That happened quite a few years ago, I believe."

"Really? Do you mean you could just open jars before, in the shop?"

"Yep. No plastic seals and childproof caps that old people have to ask their grandchildren to open for them," she smirked.

"Goodness. I hope we haven't got a madman loose in Malvern, poisoning food."

"Same here. If someone is poisoning cake, they have to have a screw loose," declared the great cake-lover Tamsin, shocked that her favourite food could be abused in this way. "What was in the scones that made them taste funny anyway?"

"Here's the really odd bit. It seems Hilda couldn't work out what it was, so she ate a whole scone from the bad batch. She felt a bit sick - and they definitely tasted nasty."

"That's nuts! She could have died!"

"But you see she couldn't take them to be tested by the health people, or they'd shut her down while they did all the tests. She depends on the money she gets from her baking to feed her family."

"Difficult. I can see that. But she has to find out how it happened, doesn't she. I mean, she can't hand-deliver every single scone. The contaminant must have got in somewhere."

"Maybe someone injected something into the scones in the shop while Rosie wasn't looking?"

"That's a bit fantastical. Maybe it was just a one-off. Washing powder got into the flour or something. Wonder if the Furies have had any problems?" She took another spoonful of her breakfast of oats, apples and goats' yogurt. "Lord, we get a lot of our food from small suppliers, artisan makers too. I wonder if we're going to wake up dead one morning," she grinned.

"It's not funny when it's their livelihood," Emerald folded her arms.

"You're right. It's not funny at all." She poked at her bowl with her spoon. "Something's put me right off my oats today."

"Well, that's an absolute first!"

"Think I'll leave this for the dogs' supper." She pushed the bowl away. "Hmm, the oats I've been eating all week. I had one of those apples yesterday. I opened a new pot of yogurt this morning for the dogs' breakfast." She turned to Emerald with a look of horror. "You don't think there's something wrong with the yogurt, do you?"

"Let me have a taste." Emerald dipped her fingertip into the yogurt in the bowl and tasted it, gazing heavenwards as she smacked her lips thoughtfully, then pulled a face. "Something definitely wrong here, I'd say."

"I've got another pot in the fridge." Tamsin jumped up to fetch it, with a couple of clean spoons. They each had a taste.

"Seems fine to me," said Emerald.

"And me. Here, what does it say on the labels?" They compared the labels on the two pots. "Yeah, they're different batches. So I guess that was a one-off. Odd."

"What are you up to today, Tamsin?"

"You know what, I have a home visit on the road towards Little

Malvern. Someone got one of those fashionable 'designer dog' mongrels that's a walking vet bill. Wants private lessons. More money than sense, I'd say. But the thing is, I could drop in on The Furies on the way back. I bet they'd have some thoughts on this."

"They've been in business for years, haven't they?"

"They have. And they're like Charity, only a three-headed version. There's not much that happens that they don't know about."

"And you'll be able to find out about their latest creation!"

"I could volunteer my services as a one-woman tasting panel, yes," Tamsin smiled, as she got up from the table and started preparing her bag for her puppy visit.

CHAPTER THREE

True to her word, after her lesson with the people with the super-expensive but poorly-bred fashionable dog, where she spent a lot of time trying to persuade them that all dogs were much the same and they didn't need special food or special training for their darling, Tamsin pulled the Top Dogs van up in front of the old Malvern Ragstone Victorian villa backing into the woods on the Hills. She winced as the handbrake made its familiar squawk and looked at the headquarters of Dodds & Co. She noticed a pair of little birds splashing in the birdbath in the front garden, and realised they probably didn't have much of a back garden, the house being built right into the hill. The hot sun was still reaching the house as it was yet early in the day, lightening the brown stone. Later, when the sun dropped behind the Hills it would be cool. I suppose that's a plus for this house, she thought to herself. But in the winter it must get pretty damp, I bet. Just as well they do all that baking to dry the place out!

"Tamsin!" It was Damaris who opened the door, hopping from tiny foot to tiny foot, like the birds in their birdbath. "How lovely to see you! To what do we owe the pleasure?" And she welcomed her in while turning to call her sisters, "Penelope! Electra dear! We have a special visitor."

Electra fluttered into the hallway, while Penelope boomed from the house kitchen, "Do we need an extra cup, Damaris?"

"Oh definitely," Electra's quiet voice relayed to her sister. "Come in, Tamsin, do!"

And in no time she was seated once more in the Furies' living room, a room which appeared to be frozen in time. What time, Tamsin was none too sure, but it had a museum-like quality, not least because of all the shelves and display cabinets containing knick-knacks and souvenirs from many an English seaside town. "Did you visit all these places?" she asked as her fingers ran along the shelf bearing little china models of bathing beauties with real lace to cover their porcelain shame, an old sweet shop with buckets and spades hanging outside, and a tiny cream jug bearing the legend, 'Greetings from Hastings'.

"We most certainly did, my dear," declaimed Penelope, who always spoke as if from the pulpit. "Our parents didn't have much spare, but they were insistent we should get a holiday every August. And it was always the seaside. My mother would pretend it was the Aegean."

"We loved it!" added Electra in her floaty voice, as usual on pouring duties while Damaris handed round the cups. "It was such a totally different experience from these Hills and fields where we lived."

"I bet the beaches are full at the moment, in this heatwave," Tamsin offered, as she wondered at how the three sisters were so very different from each other. Perhaps that's why they've stayed together and run a successful business, she mused.

"It is hot, isn't it. Though we keep this room cool." Penelope gestured to the thick brown velvet curtains, drawn across most of the bay windows, the ancient cream lace curtains peeping out between the gaps. "Back in the day, in *our* day, it was beautifully sunny every day," declaimed Penelope in her deep voice.

"And there were thunderstorms every night," piped up Damaris enthusiastically, her small childlike voice such a contrast to her big sister's.

"That's the time for them!" laughed Tamsin, marvelling at people's ability to re-paint the past in radiant colours, where perhaps there were none. "I love a good thunderstorm. Freshens everything up."

"I love hearing the thunder rolling along the top of the Hills," said Electra dreamily.

"Does it frighten your dogs, Tamsin?" asked Damaris with concern.

"Fortunately we don't get enough thunderstorms for it to be an issue - but I do what I do for fireworks. Shut the place down, turn the telly up loud, play games with them."

"You have a special bond with your animals," this from Electra, nodding slowly.

"Now, my dear. Cake," interrupted Penelope. "We're going to use you as a guinea pig. We have a new recipe we're working on. Want your opinion."

"Oh, how exciting!" Tamsin clapped her hands together. "Your cakes are all marvels."

"Is that why you came?" Penelope winked and Tamsin blushed.

"No, it's not why I came, but a girl can hope?" and gratefully accepted the plate Electra handed to her. The cake was dark, moist, and covered with thick coffee-coloured icing, with long chocolate curls on top.

Tamsin decided to give her full attention to this offering, and delivered her verdict mostly in mono-syllables and sounds. "Mmm, Oh wow, so good! Mmmmm," And finally, "When can I get this at The Cake Stop?"

"I'll be delivering next Tuesday," said Damaris.

"Can't wait. But tell me, I didn't come by just to scrounge cake. I did have something I wanted to ask you. Have you heard about Hilda and her scones?"

"We have. Awful, really awful."

"Such a lovely lady - a really good home cook." Was Penelope damning Hilda with faint praise, wondered Tamsin?

"We know most of the local bakers, you see," said Damaris. "She rang up in a state, wanting to know if we had any advice for her."

"And had you?"

"We told her to report it. Tell the police."

"But she wouldn't," sighed Penelope, pouring more tea. "She thinks she'll get closed down if she does."

"It's not fair, is it - though I quite see how seriously the authorities would view it." Tamsin sipped her tea. "What kind of a nut would do this, anyway?"

Penelope spoke, "Well you know, there was something like this that happened before. Ooh, many years ago now. Before we were born - that tells you how long ago it was," she smiled lopsidedly. "People were buying from that bakery that used to be down in Malvern Link."

".. And when they cut into the bread they found rusty old bolts in it!" said Electra.

"Oh, I remember now - I'd quite forgotten!" Damaris sat up straight in her chair. "Wasn't it an act of revenge?"

"Yes, turns out it was a disgruntled employee who'd been given the sack. There was still rationing from the war, and working in a bakery was a plum job as there were always bits to be got 'under the counter'. They were also exempt from military service if they worked in a bakery."

"Wow - great incentive to keep your bakery job! And while the person was working off her notice, she put stuff in the bread?"

"That's right! Bolts, clothes pegs, even a plug on a chain! Nothing that people were likely to swallow, like a needle. She didn't want to kill anyone, just destroy the bread and get the baker in awful trouble."

"Surely she was caught easily enough?"

"She was. But it caused no end of fuss for the shop. If it hadn't been for rationing and all the food shortages people probably would have avoided the shop. But they couldn't really."

"Times were hard."

"Oh, they were. We can't imagine it these days. My mother used to tell me about baking cakes with vinegar instead of eggs,"

".. and carrots instead of sugar!" said Damaris. "Carrot cake's a luxury now, though they do put sugar in it as well these days."

"So," Tamsin thought out loud, "I wonder if Hilda has really upset someone? Someone who wants her shut down? It's so different these days, with all the Health and Safety inspectors crawling all over the place."

"We're always being tested," said Electra airily. "Always seem to have people taking samples of this and that."

"Wouldn't Hilda have visits too?"

"She would. Her set-up has to have passed muster or she wouldn't be able to sell anything at all."

"I can see why she doesn't want to involve the authorities. I guess she's hoping it was a one-off. Gosh, supposing it happens again?"

"She'll have to do something. I wonder if you're right, Tamsin - that someone wants to get at her."

"Either that or they're bats in the belfry," said Damaris.

"Or working with the dark side," said Electra mysteriously.

They were all quiet for a moment.

"I can tell you we've upped all our security measures since we heard," Penelope put her cup and saucer down on the tea tray. "We taste every new bag of ingredients we open. And Damaris does the delivering, so until the cakes arrive with the customer, nothing can go wrong with them."

"Something could go wrong afterwards though?" Tamsin offered. "I mean some nut could put something into the cake in the shop, when no-one's looking?"

"That's true. But what can we do? If that happened with Hilda, it's easy to imagine. The Farmers' Market gets very busy, there could be all sorts of goings-on in the pushing and shoving."

"Poor Hilda."

The sisters all nodded sagely, thankful that it hadn't happened to them.

CHAPTER FOUR

Tamsin was careful to use the new pot of yogurt for her breakfast and to give to the dogs. "Only the best for you my preciouses!" she said, as she gave them each a spoonful. "And," she added, as Emerald swung her legs down from the kitchen wall where she'd been doing a headstand for what seemed an age, "I think we should talk to Susannah. She puts her life and soul into her products. We should tell her. I really think she'd want to know. *I'd* want to know if one of the harnesses I sold in class fell apart - I really would!"

"I think you're right. Seeing as what's happened to Hilda. I think we should. I could do with some more cheese anyway. You free this morning?"

"Got a 10 o'clock - but it's only in Cowleigh. Pick you up at 11.15?"

And by quarter to twelve, with the sun beating down on the van as they struggled up the bockety lane, they rolled into the yard and parked.

"Marigold, you're done," said Susannah as she led a splendid large white goat out of one of the sheds towards the pasture gate. "Oh hello again! Just doing some hooves today," she nodded to Marigold's neat feet as she slipped the hand-plaited collar off the goat's long neck and shoo-ed her into the field. "What can I do for you this glorious day?"

"More yogurt please," Tamsin smiled brightly. "Why do you take the collar off?"

"Oh, the others would chew it to bits," Susannah laughed. "'Know your enemy', remember?"

"And more of your beautiful cheese," said Emerald, lifting the shopping basket out of the side of the van.

"And there's a tiny problem," Tamsin wasn't sure how to broach the subject, but Susannah abruptly stopped in her progress to the dairy, turned and said, "Oh?"

So Tamsin told her about the yogurt tasting distinctly odd. "The van's pretty cool and we went straight home from here, so it was in the fridge within minutes rather than hours. I brought the pot with me, in case you want to check the batch or something."

Susannah's face crumpled and she slumped against the wall. "Oh no. What's happening? You're the second person to complain. A customer came up yesterday - a new customer. Said 'if this is what goats' yogurt tastes like I don't want it'. I gave her her money back of course, straight away, but I have to confess I thought she'd left her shopping in the car too long. Cars get boiling hot very fast in this sun."

"Who're you telling?" Tamsin gave a short laugh, "I'm always telling dog-owners this."

"But that's not what happened here." She sniffed the pot and took a small taste off the end of her finger. "This doesn't taste like bacteria - more a chemical sort of taste ... This is awful! I'll have to withdraw that batch from sale and get it tested. Er, thank you for taking the trouble to bring me the pot. I just need to confirm the label is the same batch as the other customer's." She sighed loudly and put her hands over her face for a moment.

"How could it have got contaminated?" asked Tamsin.

"I'm just wondering exactly that. Customers usually are served at the front of the dairy here, where we are. It's like a mini-shop."

"Well, we can't get at any of your dairy proper," Emerald peered round the big display fridge at the shiny stainless steel equipment beyond.

"Ohhhh," groaned Susannah. "I had an Open Day a week ago. Loads of people. I spent a lot of time making sure the children didn't chase the kids. Never thought anyone would creep into the dairy and do something nefarious."

They were silent for a moment, and Tamsin nodded to Emerald.

"Did you hear about Hilda? At the Farmers' Market?" Emerald asked quietly.

Susannah emerged from behind her hands with a sigh. "No?"

"She supplies the *Health in the Hills* with bakery. Some scones tasted funny this week and Linda had to return them."

"Oh no! Have we got a maniac on the loose?" gasped Susannah.

"Hilda seems to think so," said Tamsin.

"It seems she's as fanatical as you are about hygiene and sticking to the rules," said Emerald. "She's gone over and over it and can't see how anything can have gone wrong her end."

"If someone's adding something to the products after they've been made, how can they be doing it? That's the question!" Tamsin always wanted to look forward and solve problems rather than dwell on them. "Give me that pot again."

She grabbed the pot she'd brought back and studied it carefully. She snapped off the lid and ran her finger round the rim. "Yes!" she said with triumph. "Look here - there's a tiny, tiny hole just up under the lid."

They all peered at where she was pointing.

"And inside?" asked Emerald.

"Inside there's a rough bit. Look!" and Tamsin showed them the corresponding bit of sharp plastic.

"A tiny needle!" exclaimed Susannah. "Someone injected the pot with a tiny syringe!" and she followed this with a few choice words to describe the evil-doer.

"Was this the only batch you had on the shelves at your Open Day?"

"Yes. I always keep the next batch in a separate fridge till the whole previous batch is sold." And she fled to the fridge to check the date-stamps on the remaining stock. "There's only a dozen or so of that batch left." She took all the big pots and carried them over to the counter so they could check them. They each grabbed a pot to get started.

"Here! Here's a hole!" said Tamsin and put the pot aside and picked up another.

"Can't see one here .." Emerald turned the pot round and round, peering under the edge of the lid.

"This one's got a hole," said Susannah through gritted teeth, snapping off the lid, sniffing the yogurt, then running her finger over the inside by the hole. "Yep. I can feel it." More expletives followed. "I'm sorry, I don't usually swear,"

"You're ok! I'd swear if it were me. This pot's ok." Tamsin took another.

And between them they found four of the pots had holes, just under the lid. "When you add in the two that we know about, that's at least six that were got at. How long would it take to do, I wonder?"

"Not long if you were good at it. You could practice piercing plastic pots all day till you had the knack."

"And injecting scones would be very easy. And quick."

"We *have* got a nutcase abroad," Emerald said glumly.

"But why? Even a madman has some sort of reason," Tamsin was matter-of-fact, as ever.

"Someone with a grudge against small businesses?"

"Particularly artisan makers?"

"Someone who wants to put you all out of business?"

"How about," said Tamsin, looking devious, "someone who wants to target one artisan in particular, and is clouding the issue by doing a lot of you?"

Susannah shivered. "I'd like to think there isn't anyone who wants to put me in particular out of business." And she folded her arms.

"A smokescreen," said Emerald thoughtfully. "So far we've only found nasty tastes. No-one seems to be any the worse for the scones or the yogurt. They're not trying to kill anyone."

"Unless the smokescreen is bigger than we think!"

"Oh Tamsin, you always think the worst!" said a shocked Emerald.

"Haven't I good reason to? Haven't we seen a lot of the worst in people over the last year or so?" And to Susannah she said, "Susannah. Damage limitation. Do you keep a list of customers? So you can approach them and offer a replacement if necessary?"

"I don't, no. People just wander in when they see the goats. Or they know where to come, like you did. And I supply shops too."

"Which ones?"

"Well, there's Linda's *Health in the Hills* for one. And there's a strange little place on the Gloucester Road. One in Hereford ... oh, and one in Worcester. I wonder if I should speak to them? It's such a worry - if they haven't heard anything, then I'll be worrying them unduly and they'll cancel their orders anyway."

"You're in a cleft stick," Tamsin nodded. "I think you need to sit down and think about what to do with them. Perhaps start with one you have a great relationship with? Do any of them do Farmers' Markets?"

"I don't believe so. Some do fairs, and there are a few coming up in August. Oh dear ... I know what. I'll talk to Michael - he runs the Hereford shop. Wise old bird. And he's carried my goats' products for a few years now."

"That would be a great starting point," nodded Emerald encouragingly. "He'll know it's not your stuff that's at fault. And we need to visit the Farmers' Market - see if anyone else is affected."

"Great idea, Girl Wonder," laughed Tamsin. "You're beginning to think like me!"

"I really hope not," mumbled Emerald, and grinned demurely. "But this has to be investigated."

"And Hilda won't report it. What sort of testing will you do, Susannah?"

"I'll send it to a different lab. The whole batch was tested in the vat and came up clear. It's nothing the Department should be concerned about - from the food-health point of view, I mean. It's clearly something introduced afterwards."

"You really don't want to mess with the authorities, do you."

"Once you start a hare like that, they'll be in here every day! The very thought makes me nervous. You know, when I was setting up and they came to inspect the premises they said I had to have a separate wash hand basin for employees. I told them I had no employees, that it was only me, and eventually they let it rest. You can see I wash everything all the time - the floor's still wet from this morning. It has to dry naturally - pretty quick in this weather! Oh, and they wanted me to install a toilet in the dairy too. Quite mad!"

"I see what you mean! We'll do some sniffing around. There may be others who've been affected."

"And one of *them* may be prepared to report it, officially," added Emerald, surprised to find herself excited at the prospect of a bit more detecting.

CHAPTER FIVE

One of the joys of rural towns is the preponderance of street markets. And Great Malvern was no exception, with its Craft market one Saturday a month alternating with the hugely-popular Farmers' Market on the other Saturdays.

When Tamsin and Emerald arrived after lunch, with Quiz and Moonbeam in tow - Banjo would not enjoy the bustle of a market - it was crowded and busy with lots of chatter and laughter. Two musicians were stationed at one end of the row of covered stalls with their gay green-striped rooves, playing folk music on a variety of instruments. Tamsin watched as they put down the pipes and tabor and selected a flute and a fiddle for their next piece.

The July sun was beating down on the happy scene, as some stall-holders moved their produce around to keep it out of the sun, draping cloths across their stands, and others had just a few items on show with notices explaining that there was plenty more in their cool-boxes. Some had small fridges whirring away on their tables.

The visitors were delighted with the sunny day, and the scent of the warm bread from the bakery stands was intoxicating. Tamsin and Emerald filled their shopping bags first of all - Emerald got wholemeal bread, honey and oil, while Tamsin carried the green beans, salad, tomatoes, and some delicious-looking early corn on the cob, their brown tassels and green leaves poking out of the top of the bag.

"I've gone a bit mad here," said Tamsin ruefully, swinging the bag over her shoulder. "It'll weigh twice as much by the time we get home."

"We should make a little trailer for Quiz to pull," laughed Emerald, admiring her granary loaf peeping out of her smaller bag.

"Hear that, Quiz? She wants to put you to work!" Quiz waved her tail happily, as she greeted a couple of children who were Ooh-ing and Aah-ing over her and little Moonbeam, who amused them hugely by standing underneath Quiz, her head peeping out between the bigger dog's legs.

"Did you find anything out yet?" asked Tamsin quietly.

"Nobody's said anything - not sure how to ask them!"

"Oh, hey, look at that! *The Cider Flagon*. Haven't seen him before. Let's go have a shufti."

They admired the different sized bottles with their elegant labelling in black and gold, and were leaning over to read the large coloured posters hanging at each end of the stand when the Cider man himself - tall and tanned with a head of dark hair - finished serving his customer and welcomed them with a cheery smile.

"This is fascinating," Tamsin pointed to the poster. "How long have you been doing this?"

"I've been messing about making cider for friends for a few years, but commercially - just over a year. As soon as it becomes a business you have to toe the line with regard to all the legislation and whatnot."

"So I gather! And where are you - it says 'deepest Hereford' here."

"Here's a map for you," he directed them to another big poster at the other end of the stall. "That's the farmhouse, and all these orchards around it are where the apples come from." He proudly patted the basket of cider apples beside one of the large bottles.

Tamsin peered at the map. "Oh, I know where that is! I walk my dogs there sometimes," she pointed to the orchard where she and her pathologist friend Maggie would meet from time to time to walk together. "I have a friend who lives nearby."

"Someone who lives nearby with a dog and who walks in my orchards? Hmm, that wouldn't be the two doctors at Canal House by any chance?"

"That's them! Maggie and Don, and their old dog Jez. You know them?"

"It's very rural, so we all know our neighbours," he smiled easily. "I must tell them I met you when I next run into them. What's your name?" He tilted his head with the question.

"Tamsin! Tamsin Kernick. And you're …?"

"Jonathan. Mapley, Jonathan Mapley."

"You don't mind people walking in your orchards?" she asked tentatively.

"Not at all - they're lovely and the occasional walker and dog does no damage. It's nice that others can enjoy them. And yours are such beautifully behaved dogs!" he beamed at Moonbeam and Quiz who were both silently eyeing a droopy-eared Basset Hound, looking very bored as his owners studied the fare at the next stand.

"That's kind - thank you! Have you been there long?"

"Born there. My parents had the orchards but sold the apples on. I still sell some while I build up my production. And I've just started in this market too - this is my first week … oh hallo, what's going on here?"

Raised voices had interrupted them. "Well it's just not fair!" said a complaining voice. And a calmer, quieter, one, from someone who was clearly trying to pour oil on troubled waters, said, "It was a committee decision. You're free to apply again next year."

"I don't want to apply again next year. I want to have a stand now. You're just looking after your cronies - you don't want to give a new person a chance."

"That simply isn't so, Mr. Curtin. There are a few new people here. But they all had to go through the same selection process. We have strict guidelines - and we have to limit the numbers of similar products offered.

It's better for the makers and it's definitely better for the customers. And, as you know, we already have two metalworkers in the craft market."

"Blow your guidelines! And blow your carefully selected new people. This isn't the end of this! I'm telling you," he wagged a finger, "you haven't heard the last of me!" And Mr. Curtin turned on his heel and stomped away, not forgetting to glower at Jonathan as he went.

"Phew!" said the lady who had been trying to appease Mr. Curtin. "Sometimes this job is hard."

"You ok, Felicity?" asked Jonathan quietly.

"Yes thanks, Jonathan. Sorry that had to happen in front of your stand on your first day."

"No worries. People can get easily upset."

"You get back to your customers," she smiled at Tamsin and Emerald and glided off between the stands, the crowd of curious onlookers having dissipated now the entertainment seemed to be over. Felicity spoke to the musicians and they immediately struck up a rousing dance piece, with lots of tabor and whoops of excitement to distract the visitors.

Tamsin bade goodbye to Jonathan and set off down the market again, drawing the two dogs in to follow behind her and swinging her shopping bag merrily.

"Is Hilda here?" Tamsin peered down the length of market stalls. "Yes - there she is, down at the end, opposite *The Crusty Loaf.*"

"*Hilda's Homebakes.*" Emerald read the sign hanging over the stall. "Let's go and talk to her. If anyone knows anything, she will. Wonder if she knows anything about the disgruntled Mr. Curtin?" Emerald started walking.

"And we must buy something from her - show solidarity, you know."

It wasn't hard for them to buy from Hilda, as she had Lemon Curd on offer as well as her usual cakes and scones.

"Oh Lemon Curd! I love homemade Lemon Curd!" said Tamsin, picking up the jar. "Hey, has this got one of those tamperproof lids on?" she asked, pointing to the dip in the metal lid.

"No dear," said Hilda. "It's just what happens when the hot curd or jam cools down in the jar. It kind of sucks the lid in. It'll pop when you first open it."

"There's nothing new under the sun!" laughed Tamsin, offering her money and handing the jar to Emerald as her own shopping bag was crammed.

"We're friends of Linda's, you know - from *Health in the Hills?*"

"Ah. So that's why you were asking about tamperproof lids," said Hilda glumly.

"It's something at the front of my mind at the moment. You see," Tamsin spoke very quietly, so no-one in the milling crowds could over-hear. "Linda told us about the awful goings-on with your scones."

"She did?" Hilda looked alarmed.

"Only because she thought we may be able to help," Emerald assured her. "We do understand that it's hard to go public on this."

Hilda put half a dozen scones into a bag for a customer, smiled happily as she gave them their change, and turned back to Tamsin. "Come round the back of the stall. I don't want anyone listening in." She lifted the awning at the side of the stall and beckoned them through. They squeezed in between the plastic crates of bakes and Hilda's stool.

"I've been so upset about it. But it seems that Linda's scones were the only ones affected."

"Well, that's a blessing. They were interfered with in the shop, you mean?"

"I'm sure of it. You could eat your dinner off my kitchen floor, never mind the worktops!"

"So," ventured Tamsin, "do you know if this has happened to anyone else?"

"That's just the thing. The baker over there - Malcolm, he had a couple of bread-rolls brought back - his ciabatta ones. They had a funny taste, the customer said - just like my scones had."

"What sort of taste was it?"

"Sort of metallic. Not like something gone off, know what I mean?"

"Hmm. So someone had a go at Malcolm's bread rolls. Anyone else?"

"It's hard to say with the fruit and veg. People wouldn't probably bring them back. They'd think there was something wrong with their saucepan or something. But Gary - he's the guy with the potatoes and cabbages over there," she nodded towards the laden stall next to Malcolm's, "he says he's hardly sold any of his young carrots this week. Last week they were flying out."

"People voting with their feet," pondered Tamsin.

"I see what you mean," said Emerald. "They just think the carrots don't taste nice."

"Tell me Hilda, did you hear that rumpus going on a little while ago?"

"That Curtin fellow? I did. He's a right pain. He applied to the market weeks ago and was refused. And he keeps coming back and complaining ..."

"I *told* her it couldn't be the wool!" They heard a distressed voice in the thoroughfare between the stalls. "But I had to give her her money back - she was so cross!"

"What's happening here?" Tamsin nodded towards Malcolm's bakery stand.

"That's Carmel - from *Sheep's Clothing* down the end. She's really upset! I'm going to see what's up." And Hilda marched out from the back of her stall and put a hand on Carmel's elbow while she leaned in to talk to her.

Not sure whether they were meant to be minding the shop, Tamsin turned to Emerald with her finger to her lips and slid out to join the group in front of the bread stall.

"It was my best fine Shetland lace shawl - my most expensive item," Carmel was complaining.

"I heard you celebrating!" said Malcolm.

"I was! Thought I'd covered my market expenses for a month with that sale. The shawls are made with my own wool, of course, from my own flock. First I spin the wool, then knit it. They take ages to make as they're just one-ply."

"I know dear, I've often admired you working at one on a Saturday," Hilda was trying to calm the distraught stall-holder.

"So she bought it this morning. She was going to a wedding in the

Abbey there, and hadn't realised it would be so cold in the church when it's so boiling hot out here," she mopped her brow with the back of her hand.

"So what's the problem?" asked Malcolm, who had shifted Carmel and Hilda along to the end of his stand while he served a customer. Tamsin's ears were on stalks as she listened while admiring the beautiful loaves and ciabatta rolls, and thinking how easy it would be to jab a needle into them.

"She just came back," Carmel sounded as if she was going to cry. "And she handed back the bag with the shawl in and showed me her arms. They were awful! All red and blotchy. A horrible rash! I told her it couldn't be the wool .. I only use natural soap for the final washing, not detergent. But you should have heard what she said!"

Carmel sniffed noisily and reached for a hanky. "She threatened to report me! To Trading Standards." Malcolm and Hilda looked suitably shocked and impressed. "I couldn't risk that, so I gave her her money back. I don't know if she's suddenly developed a wool allergy or what, but I just couldn't risk it."

"I wonder .." said Hilda, glancing at Malcolm. "I wonder if you should get the shawl tested. I know your knitteds are gorgeous - and no-one's ever complained before, have they."

"No," sniffed Carmel, now weeping and dabbing her eyes with the hanky.

"Maybe someone did something to it, while it was on your stall? Was it hanging up?"

"No. It was folded. There was a pale blue one on display, but the lady preferred the cream one."

"And that was folded up? At the front of the stand?"

"Near the front - just below the hanging one."

"So anyone could have reached it, and interfered with it!" Hilda folded her arms across her ample bosom.

"But why? Why would anyone want to 'interfere with it' as you put it?"

Hilda lowered her voice. "It's not just you, Carmel. There've been other incidents. It seems we have a hater abroad - someone who wants to put artisans and creators out of business."

"That's sick!" Carmel shuddered, her tears forgotten and replaced with a righteous anger. "If I find out who did this ..."

"We don't know that anyone did anything yet, dear. Get the shawl tested. I'm sure someone here can give you the address of a lab - one that they've used. They'll get to the bottom of it."

"Suppose they can't find anything?"

"Well that would suggest that your customer has suddenly developed an allergy to wool, or whatever you washed the shawl in."

Carmel looked downhearted. "I'd better get back to my stand," she said, as she looked over and saw a few people admiring her garments. "Thanks for listening, Hilda." And she walked slowly away for a few steps, then put her shoulders back and stepped forward smartly to her stand, ready to give her audience a friendly greeting. Malcolm had lost interest and was busy serving his customers, so Hilda and Tamsin went back to Hilda's stand.

"I sold three of those buns for you, and a lardy cake," chirruped Emerald, holding out a fistful of money. "Hope I did it right?"

Hilda took the money and put it in the pouch of her money-belt, then dropped some large peanut biscuits into a bag and handed them to Emerald with a smile, before setting about re-arranging the bakes on her stand.

Tamsin whispered to Emerald, "For one who eschews commerce, you are showing quite a gift!" Then out loud she said, "Hilda, thanks for explaining all this for us. It looks as though the perpetrator is getting imaginative. Do you think they sprinkled itching powder in that shawl? It would be easy enough to chuck some in to the folds."

"And it's all so lacy - it would have spread through quickly."

"That's a point! I'm going to go and see if any spilt on her tablecloth," and she and Emerald hurried away to the *Sheeps' Clothing* stand. After the group of people admiring the display moved away, Tamsin said, "Carmel - I'm a friend of Hilda's. Show me where your cream shawl was."

Carmel, who in her distress hadn't noticed Tamsin at Malcolm's stand, looked flustered and dumbly pointed to an empty space beneath a hanging blue shawl.

"Look, there are crumbs there - a powdery substance - can you see?"

Carmel picked up the glasses hanging round her neck, perched them on her nose and peered. She pinched some of the powder between finger and thumb and rubbed it.

"I wouldn't do that!" Tamsin held out her hand to stop her, but was too late.

"Ouch!" squawked Carmel, looking at her fingers. They were already going red as she flapped her hand vigorously. "That poor woman - having this on her bare arms!"

"I'm glad she's not a monster any more, anyway," smiled Tamsin. "And I hope the rash subsided quickly so she could enjoy the wedding reception."

"I won't need to send the shawl to the lab now anyway. I have to clear this mess up!"

"You'd better check all the other garments too - give them all a shake over the cloth and see if anything comes out."

"Thank you dear, thank you for helping me. I"m just a small sheep-farmer with a love of wool. I can't understand mischief-making like this."

"No more can any of the others who've been targeted. They're all just doing what they love and trying to eke a living from it. And I do know just what it's like when that slender living is threatened by .. a nutcase."

"Oh - I've just realised," said Carmel, for the first time noticing the dogs patiently standing beside Tamsin. "You're that dog trainer that solves murders. How do you keep finding them to solve?"

"I don't," wailed Tamsin. "They find me! And I so wish they wouldn't."

"Anyway," Emerald interjected, "this is just a nut with a grudge. This isn't a murder."

How soon that was to change!

CHAPTER SIX

Tamsin and Emerald walked Quiz and Moonbeam back home, taking a detour on to the Common and keeping as much as possible in the shade of the great trees. They stopped at the stream so that the dogs could lie down in it to cool off while the women sat on the little footbridge swinging their legs, glad to put down their laden shopping bags for a while. When the dogs were thoroughly wet, Quiz lying first on one side then on the other to make sure the water reached everywhere, they hopped off the bridge and shrieked and danced as the dogs shook and splashed water all over their legs.

"Thanks dogs! Now I'm cooled off too!" laughed Tamsin as she looked down at the dark splash marks on her shorts as they headed home.

"How come you hardly got wet?" asked Emerald, who was shaking the water off her skirt.

"There's a trick to it!" Tamsin chuckled. "You have to stand at the sharp end, right in front of their nose. The water mostly goes flying off to either side."

"Ohh! Thanks, I'll remember that for next time," Emerald said ruefully as she flapped her skirt. "They're spreading the water around without having to carry it," said Emerald. "How about we do a bit of spreading? Spreading the word, I mean. Splash some info in the right direction? Those makers are all too frightened of the authorities to report all this to the police."

"Great idea! And I know just what you're thinking ... it involves the *Malvern Mercury*, am I right?"

"Exactly. We know we can trust Feargal not to name the victims or point any fingers. Maybe it'll frighten off the lunatic who's doing this."

"We'll call him when we get back. Actually I haven't seen him for an age - let's ask him round tomorrow to eat some of this lovely grub. He's always hungry."

And so they did.

And so he was.

It took the lean and lanky young man with the head of auburn floppy curls no time at all to clean up the huge plate of sandwiches they'd made with the brown bread, lemon curd, tomatoes and lettuce they'd bought at the market.

Emerald had made lemonade and added plenty of ice which clanked in the jug as she poured three glasses and handed them round. They all stretched out in the cool North-facing living room.

"They say these are record temperatures," said Tamsin idly. "Apparently people are fleeing like lemmings to the beaches. Sitting in a hot car in a traffic jam for hours to squash onto a noisy crowded beach doesn't appeal to me one bit. We're much better off here in the Hills!"

"We're almost the furthest point from any beach here in Malvern. It's quite a trek to reach one," said Feargal. "I prefer beaches in the winter anyway, when they're empty."

"Me too!" said Tamsin settling back in her chair. "Much better for the dogs too."

"In the Winter when we're huddled round the fire I curse the fact that this room faces North," said Emerald, setting her glass down by her chair, and shooing Opal off so she could sit down. "It's too hot for laps today, Opal, sorry." And her white cat put her tail up in the air like a flagpole and strutted away.

"But we're really glad of the North-facing windows when the weather's like this!" agreed Tamsin. "No need to close the curtains - though I can tell you mine are firmly shut. My bedroom's on the other side of the house, you see, in full sun all day."

"Do they do cakes at this market, then?" asked Feargal pointedly, looking around hopefully.

Tamsin smiled as she passed him the plate of peanut biscuits. "These are made by Hilda, and that's part of why we invited you - want a story?"

Feargal stuffed most of the biscuit into his mouth and drew his notebook and pen out of his pocket with a flourish. "You bet," he mumbled through the biscuity crumbs. "Hey, this biscuit's scrumptious! Yeah, it's quiet as a morgue round here. It's the silly season and the editor's desperate for something other than flower shows and stolen shopping trolleys. They actually found one hanging from the top of one of those tall lampposts in the shopping centre the other day. Malvern louts are getting inventive!"

"Ooh, we have something much better than that!" Tamsin grinned and started to unfold the story so far to Feargal, who listened with interest and the occasional raised eyebrow as he jotted down some notes. "So you see how awful it is for these poor artisans?" she finished.

"They're like us," said Emerald, "they just want to earn an honest living, or even just pin-money, doing what they love."

"And in some cases that's involved huge investment. I'm thinking of Malcolm the baker, and the cider fella."

"And, of course, Susannah! She has this lovely smallholding, loads of goats, lots of equipment .." said Emerald.

"And she complies with all the loads of testing and inspecting that has to be done. She really is deeply invested in her business. It'll be awful if this stops her being able to sell her produce."

"So you're rallying round to help?"

"I know just what it was like when my harmless and innocent way of life was threatened," she said grimly, remembering the murder that had introduced her to Feargal in the first place.

"So do I," added Emerald glumly, thinking of when the reputation of her yoga business was in danger. "So we really feel for them."

"Got it. And how many have been affected so far?"

Tamsin counted on her fingers. "Hilda, Malcolm, Susannah. Carmel the knitter - that's all we know of so far."

"Don't forget Gary and his carrots," Emerald reminded her. "That's five."

"You're expecting more?"

"There could easily be more that haven't yet come to light. Carmel's shawl may not have been discovered for weeks, and may have been given as a present to someone else. She may never have known."

"Ok. I'll do something on this. And you don't want me to name any names."

"They're all terrified of being shut down by the authorities. And they know it's not their own product at fault - it's someone else doing it. So they're not deceiving anyone. Hey, do you think your mole could add anything in the way of information?" Tamsin said with a teasing look in her eye. She was always trying to find out more about his contact in the police - his mole - but she knew a good journalist doesn't reveal his sources.

Feargal smiled back and ran his finger across his mouth to demonstrate that his lips were zipped shut. "If no-one's reported it, the police may be blissfully ignorant of the whole thing. Tell me more about this Curtin fellow who was making trouble. I can do a bit of sniffing."

So Tamsin and Emerald between them relayed the confrontation between Felicity and Curtin. "It seems he wanted a stand for his own business. Wonder what he makes?"

"I don't think I'd want to buy anything from him!" Emerald, who couldn't abide fighting, shuddered.

"I'll see what I can find. Do a quick search online through the fruit and veg shows, and the craft events."

"How will you write about it without identifying the products involved?"

"I'm a writer, aren't I!" retorted Feargal. "O ye of little faith! Just you wait and see ..."

"The thing is, if you make enough noise, maybe the headbanger who's doing this will go to ground."

"The editor may be interested in making a campaign of it. 'Who's attacking our creators?' type of thing."

"It's the old story - someone must have seen something."

"But they don't know what they saw - the significance of it, I mean," added Emerald, as she topped up the lemonade glasses and passed the plate bearing the last biscuit to Feargal, who didn't need to be asked twice.

"It's beginning to cool down at last now the sun's dropped behind the Hills." Tamsin got up and looked out of the bay window at the shadows creeping down their hill. "Let's go for a walk!"

"Suits me!" said Feargal, who always enjoyed throwing the frisbee for Banjo.

"On one condition." They turned to look at Emerald who was looking determined. "We don't discuss this any more. Just enjoy the moment - this beautiful weather, these beautiful dogs ..."

And that's exactly what they did, enjoying the cool of the summer evening, the beauty of the dogs as they chased and leapt for their frisbees, and the pleasure they took in each others' easy company and friendship. Tamsin walked barefoot on the dew-covered grass. They left their worries for another day.

And that day came round much sooner than they expected.

CHAPTER SEVEN

Tamsin had no home visits on Monday morning, so after prepping everything for her evening class in Nether Trotley she spent some time enjoying teaching her dogs a new trick.

Emerald came down the stairs to a scene of old cardboard boxes, of every size and shape - from egg-boxes to shoe-boxes and larger ones - scattered over the floor. Three dogs sat expectantly on their beds at the side of the room. "*What* are you doing now?" she asked, as Opal padded down the stairs ahead of her, sniffed cautiously at the corner of a box labelled as cat food, and hopped up onto the counter to await her breakfast.

"Scent!" replied Tamsin, as she removed a couple of boxes and shuffled the others around. "Over a third of the dog's brain is devoted to scent."

"As opposed to yours, where at least a third is devoted to cake," grinned Emerald.

"Quite so. This is why cake is so important to me. But for dogs - it's their noses!" She touched Quiz's big muzzle fondly. "Seriously though, they have extraordinary gifts when it comes to smelling things. And they love it, don't you guys?" There were some answering tail-thuds from the two bigger dogs.

"So why all the litter all over the place. Have you been raiding the supermarket?"

"I hoard suitable boxes in the shed. Shows when you last darkened its door to get the lawn-mower!" Tamsin grinned at her friend. "It's just a way to hide the article I want them to hunt for. Moonbeam's only beginning, so I put the toy just inside one of the big boxes, on its side - open. Quiz is a whiz, as is Banjo now, so the toy may be hidden in a small box inside another box, or on a chair, or anywhere. They have to work to find it."

"Can I see? Oh, I'll just start the coffee .."

"Hang on a minute, don't want to confuse their nasal passages. I'm using catnip to scent the toy. I'll show you first, then coffee is a great plan."

And she took Quiz out of the room, came back in without her and walked around all the boxes, touching some of them, then hid the little fluffy rat inside an open box upside down in a bigger box which she closed after dropping in yet another small box. "This is a difficult one!" she said to Emerald, then called, "In you come Quiz," as she opened the door, "Find!"

The big dog's ears were pricked, her tail wagging fast as she methodically worked her way round all the boxes inhaling and exhaling loudly, occasionally snorting to clear her nose entirely of scent. At one stage her nose - as if on a string - pulled her back to a box she'd just passed until she homed in on the big box, sniffing it carefully and thoroughly. Then she sat and stared at it.

"That's her signal - good girl Quizzy!" and Tamsin opened the first box and let the dog tell her where the rat was located. "Wheee!" Tamsin opened the little box that Quiz nudged with her nose, pulled out the rat and tossed it in the air for the dog to play with, joyfully. Quiz pranced round the room on her toes, holding her find proudly up in the air.

"Why do you get them to sit? Wouldn't it be easier if they picked the rat up?"

"Contamination. In case they're doing something where it's important that nothing's disturbed, or be covered with doggy drool. I learnt that from Search & Rescue training with Banjo. You know he's going to qualify as a Cadaver Dog soon?"

"That's pretty impressive! But I wonder if we want to find any *more* dead bodies than we already do!" Emerald flipped the kettle switch to ON, and started to clatter mugs and coffee pot. "Can they find other things, that don't have catnip on them?"

"What they're doing is finding something that's out of place. So once they've got the idea of searching with their noses and not their eyes, it's easy to get them to find anything really. And they can actually sniff out lots of things - they're used as seizure alert dogs to forewarn epileptics when they're going to have a fit. They can detect cancers. They can find drugs, or money, or foodstuffs being smuggled. They're just ... amazing!"

"Amazing is right .." Emerald began, but she was interrupted by the phone ringing.

"Let it go to message, I'll deal with them all later," said Tamsin.

Emerald leaned over to read the number. "Oh, that's Susannah's number, I'm pretty sure. Wonder if she has news?" and she passed the phone to Tamsin.

And Susannah most certainly did have news!

"Hey Susannah, slow down! I can't get what you're saying." Tamsin flipped the phone to speaker so Emerald could hear their friend's stressed garbled speech.

Susannah was rushing her words, breathless and panicky. "Someone's DIED!" she squawked through the tinny speaker. "Someone's actually DIED, and the police arrived mob-handed to take my place apart."

"What were they looking for?" Tamsin spoke slowly and steadily in hopes of slowing Susannah down a bit.

"I dunno - evidence! Someone DIED. It's so awful ..." and she started to snivel.

"Hang on. Who died? And what's it got to do with you?"

"Some old woman in Great Malvern. One of those big old Victorian houses on your side of the Hills. They think she was poisoned, and apparently she's been eating loads of my yogurt lately."

"She must have eaten other stuff too. She can't have lived on your yogurt only! Why are they picking on you?"

Susannah took a deep breath and tried to keep her voice steady. "It seems she had some digestive problem and someone had suggested goats' yogurt to her. She wasn't really old and doolally - but a bit intense as they put it - so she started eating loads of it. And now she's dead!" she wailed.

"Calm down! Presumably they're going to do a post mortem to find what she died of. Then they'll test all the yogurt pots in her house and find you're in the clear." Tamsin tried to be as rational as possible in the face of the emotion flooding out of the phone speaker. She glanced at Emerald who had her hand to her face and was chewing her lip anxiously.

"But supposing they find something in the pots?" Susannah bleated. "Maybe that mad person's put something dreadful in them! Oh, it's so awful - they're going to close me down!"

"Look, put the kettle on, and go cuddle some goats. We'll be with you in twenty minutes. We'll work this out! Really Susannah - I know it seems awful now, but it'll be ok." She switched off the phone and turned to Emerald. "Can you put the coffee in beakers for the car? Let's go up and see what we can do to talk her down from the ledge."

"I feel like International Rescue!" laughed Emerald. "Did they drink much coffee?"

"Thunderbirds were made of fibreglass, so perhaps powdered glass was more their thing," Tamsin grinned back. "Looks like the team is in business again, Girl Wonder. We'll help her get it sorted. It's crazy to think she had anything to do with it."

And while they drove to Susannah's farmstead, Emerald was fiddling with her phone. "I want to see where the campaign is at in the *Mercury*. Feargal's piece this morning is good, isn't it."

"Yep," said Tamsin as she drove between the tall rock walls of the Wyche Cutting and saw the plains of Herefordshire open out before them, glowing in the hot sun. The Welsh mountains beyond were barely visible through the heat haze. "It was very clever how he managed to tell the story, make it exciting, and not actually give any information at all!"

"Mmm. People are writing comments ... let me see ... Nothing concrete. Just wild suggestions so far."

"But it's caught the public's imagination!"

"It certainly has. And now it's going to explode."

"They may not connect this death with the tampering. I doubt the police will be releasing much info as yet. They don't want to cause mass panic. Maybe they're barking up the wrong tree and the old woman died of natural causes?"

"And I know who you'll be talking to later on today ..."

"I will definitely be tapping into all my contacts." Tamsin glanced across at Emerald with a wink. "And Maggie will be the first! Here we are, at Goat Paradise. Hang on to your coffee mug for the really bouncy bit. I've finished mine." And they bounced and rollicked past the herd of white goats, curiously peering over the hedge that they were busily eating, up Susannah's dreadful drive.

CHAPTER EIGHT

Susannah looked a fright. Her hair was all over the place, there was straw caught in her overalls, and her general look was frantic. "I'm so behind today," she said as the Top Dogs van decanted its passengers. "I'm just so upset!"

"Of course." Tamsin gave her a hug. "And we're here to help you. What needs to be done?"

"Um," Susannah cast around to find something that they'd be able to do. "Oh, you could feed the kids, that would be great. You know how to do that. Here, let's get the bottles ready." She led them towards the dairy. "I haven't even finished the milking yet, I've been so thrown. Only a couple more goats to do, though."

Armed with the full bottles - and reminders to ensure they were always tipped so the kids didn't gulp air - Tamsin and Emerald went to the kids' pens, where they got a massive greeting with much bleating, the kids jostling for position at the front of the pens. It must be said, there was a certain amount of giggling while they fed the hungry kids, who made short work of their bottles.

"They're so comical!" laughed Emerald.

"I could happily work with animals all day," Tamsin said dreamily as she gave the boldest kid's head a scratch.

"You do already."

"Lucky, aren't I!"

"I wouldn't say it's luck. You've listened to your heart and you've followed it. That's how things should be."

"Now, you say it, that's what all our friends are doing."

"Birds of a feather .."

"Let's take these back and see what else we can do." Tamsin gave her friend an appreciative clap on the back as they bade the satisfied kids goodbye. And they reached the milking parlour as the last two goats were released out into the field again, scampering now their heavy udders had been emptied.

"Thank you so much!" said Susannah, looking markedly less harassed. "Mornings are pretty relentless."

"What can we do next?"

"You could give me a hand spreading fresh straw in the pens. And re-filling the hay mangers."

"Right-o! Milking all done?"

"Yes, the milk's cooling now. I'm not making cheese today - and I'm certainly not making any yogurt! So it'll all stay in the bulk tank till tomorrow. I can wash down the milking parlour later." She sighed noisily. "What a day!"

Tamsin and Emerald managed to make the straw-spreading into a game, and even got Susannah laughing.

"You can just shake it out and toss it over the kids - they'll enjoy that, and they'll leap about and flatten it soon enough," she smiled as she watched her precious kids dancing about in the straw 'rain'. "Hey, Beech-nut, you love this, don't you! And you can just slot a section of hay into each hay-rack. Be sure to clip the lid down, or they'll climb up and pull it all out on to the floor."

"Does it matter? If they're going to eat it anyway?"

"Oh no! These are goats, not cattle! They won't touch the hay if it's been on the floor."

"Goodness, I had no idea they were so fastidious!"

"They do keep their coats a lovely bright white," observed Emerald.

"Yes, they're very clean animals," nodded Susannah with pride.

Emerald had picked up on how much Susannah loved to teach, so she asked, "What else do your goats eat?" and was rewarded with a lengthy description of the way she chose to feed her animals and why. Susannah became quite animated and was visibly becoming more normal. "I feed 'straights' - oats, maize, and so on - and mix the feed myself, rather than have someone bundling who-knows-what into the bags."

"Your principles align very much with how I feed my dogs," said Tamsin thoughtfully. "Mine get a species-specific diet - not just one that's convenient for me."

"Oh yes, goats are browsers, not grazers, so I have a wild flower mix I sow into the field every year. I have to manage the field rotation so that the plants get a chance to flourish. The girls would polish off the lot before they began if they had the chance!"

"Not grazers? That's interesting."

"They actually get ill if they only have grass. Goats have a very high mineral requirement." Susannah brushed the straw off her sleeves, gave one of the kids a kiss and smiled, almost for the first time today. "Bye bye Birch, see you later Hazel."

"And what are these three called?" asked Tamsin, pointing to the kids she had been feeding earlier.

"That's Primrose at the back. Lupin is the tall one, and this nosy critter here is Dandelion." They all smiled at the sweet names.

And it was a much calmer goatkeeper who led them to the farmhouse kitchen and slid the kettle over onto the Aga hotplate. It wasn't until they were all sitting at the big scrubbed deal table that Tamsin said, "So? Give us a blow-by-blow account. When did the police call?"

"It was about 7 o'clock. I was just letting the hens out. There were four of them, two in uniform. Gave me quite a fright. I wondered what on earth could have happened. They said a woman had died and they needed to have a look round. I had no idea what they were talking about, of course. And I don't think they had much idea what they were looking for, anyway, to be honest." She shifted in her chair. "One of the detectives was very taken with the goats - kept glancing over into the goathouse - so I took them into the kids' pens, and sure enough the dear little things worked their magic and softened the official attitude. They told me that it was an old woman in Great Malvern. That she'd been eating lots of my yogurt for her stomach problems, and now she had died. Her carer found her this morning. Mabel Carstairs was the poor woman's name. I don't know who she is, and I told them that." She took a gulp of her tea. "She's not one of my regular customers, I mean."

"She could have got it from *Health in the Hills*?"

"Yes, there are a few places which carry my yogurt. At the moment." She looked bleakly at them. "Probably not for much longer."

"I told you, you're jumping ahead - don't meet trouble halfway!" Tamsin put her hand over Susannah's for a moment. "They've got to do all the testing first. Did the police take any samples or anything?"

"No. They said they'd have to get the results of the post mortem first and see if they needed samples after that. The Department does all my testing, so they'll have records. They'll see that everything's fine." She looked pleadingly at Tamsin and Emerald.

"It's going to be ok," Emerald said very quietly, with a reassuring certainty.

"I saw the *Mercury* is running a bit of a campaign about this tampering." Susannah raised an eyebrow. "What alerted them to a few funny-tasting scones and an itchy shawl, I wonder .."

"Mystery to me," Tamsin grinned. "These news-hounds find out everything."

"I thought it was interesting that no names were named. Almost as if someone is protecting the makers."

"It does look like that, doesn't it." Tamsin fidgeted with her teaspoon. "So what happened next?"

"Well, nothing really. They didn't tell me any more details. They only told me her name because they wanted to see if I knew her. When they left, the nice detective who loved the kids said they probably wouldn't need to bother me again."

"They must have liked the look of the place - how clean the dairy is and all that?" said Emerald, always ready to look on the bright side.

"There you go!" said Tamsin, getting up from the table. "It'll all be ok. Maybe she just had a dodgy ticker and she died of old age? Now I have to get ready for a training session after lunch. You're all set here now?"

"Oh, thank you so much for coming to my aid! I really didn't know what I was doing .."

"Glad to have been able to help. And the kids paid us, with their antics!" Tamsin smiled over at Emerald, who echoed her smile.

"They are a delight! I think I'd spend all day with them."

"Great time-wasters, you're right. I'll deal with the milking parlour and go and soothe my soul with my goats." She gave them a warm hug and walked them out to the van. "I know you have your ear to the ground. You will let me know what you find out?"

"We will," Tamsin assured her as she opened the van, glad she'd left the windows wide open so the seats wouldn't burn them when they got in.

"Ooh, wait!" Susannah ran into the dairy and emerged a moment later with a large wedge of cheese. "Here you go, I know you like it."

Emerald took the cheese, giving Susannah's hand a squeeze, and they set off again down the bockety drive.

"Know what I need after that morning of hard labour?" Tamsin looked over to her passenger.

"Cake?"

"Cake. Let's drop in on Jean-Philippe and find out what he's heard."

"Great plan," said Emerald, taking a farewell glance at the goats. Some of the younger ones had trotted down alongside the hedge, bucking and kicking in excitement as the van drove down the hill. "They're curious."

"Like us!" Tamsin laughed.

CHAPTER NINE

"Well, *bonjour* stranger!" said a deep French voice as Tamsin ogled the cakes on offer.

"Haven't I been here recently?" asked Tamsin. "No wonder I'm desperate for cake! What have the Furies furnished for us today?"

"They've excelled themselves," Jean-Philippe smiled. "And, *en plus*, they do not taste funny."

"Oh. You're following the story in the *Malvern Mercury?*" asked Emerald.

"Not only in the paper - it's all the buzz in here." Jean-Philippe added some inventive latte art to their coffees. "Which cake have you decided on?"

"Oh - I'll have the Lemon Meringue please. Want to share?" she said to Emerald, who seldom had a whole cake herself, thereby retaining her sylph-like figure for her yoga. "When you've served these people behind us, come and tell us 'the buzz'."

"I knew you'd be in this up to your necks," the barista grinned as he added a rather hefty helping of the Meringue to their tray, with two forks. "I'll come over *en deux minutes*." Tamsin flashed her card over the little machine, and he turned to the next folk in the queue, "Good morning, *bienvenue,* how may I help you?"

"He's in fine form today," Tamsin lowered the tray carefully to her favourite table in the window.

"He loves these mysteries as much as you do!" said Emerald, settling herself in one of the armchairs, swishing her long blonde hair back over her shoulder. She leant forward and plucked a strand of hay from Tamsin's hair, "Here!"

And sure enough it was not long before Jean-Philippe came over and joined them. "People have talked of little else," he explained. "Some are even refusing to eat anything. My sales are down," he added sadly. "The sooner the *méchant* is uncovered, the better."

"And what are people saying? Anyone got anything useful? It's the sort of thing that can get worse before it's stopped."

"And you're intent on doing the stopping? I thought you'd have a hand in this somewhere!"

"These people are like us - they're just using their gifts to try to earn an honest crust. It isn't fair that some nutcase Is spoiling what they're doing."

"You're right. *Absolument.* But I haven't heard anything of value. Just people worried. But I think you may have more luck any minute now .." He nodded to the street outside the big window. "Look who's just spotted you!"

And they followed his gaze to see a slim little old lady, her face framed with her bobbed grey hair, cheerily waving at them through the glass, a small brown dog at her side. "Charity!" exclaimed Tamsin, and mouthed, "Come in!" to her as she waved back.

Jean-Philippe jumped up and with a grand Gallic flourish offered his seat to Charity, who made her way through the café to join them, slowed down by having to greet almost everyone individually as she came through the tables. The little dog had spotted Tamsin and strained on her lead to reach her. "Muffin!" called Tamsin, and Charity dropped the lead and let the dog scamper over to leap on Tamsin's lap where they had a joyful reunion as if they'd been parted for a year and not the few days since her last class in Nether Trotley.

"My dear!" said Charity as she arrived and smiled sweetly at Jean-Philippe, still holding the chair out from the table. "Have you heard?" She sat down and Muffin bounced off Tamsin's lap and onto Charity's armchair and lay down in the space beside her slender owner. "Oh thank you dear, yes, my usual tea please," to Jean-Philippe. She took out some coins then stuffed her handbag down beside her on the chair and announced in her most confidential voice, "There's been a death. And I have an awful feeling it's a *murder!*"

CHAPTER TEN

"You see," encouraged by the open-mouthed stares of her audience, Charity explained, "Dorothy rang me this morning. You know Dorothy, dear, with the B&B? It's about the squares I promised to crochet for the blankets - for the Middle Eastern refugees, don't you know?"

Tamsin nodded, wondering just how much pleasure Charity got from her 'little old lady' routine, teasing her stories out.

"And *she'd* just heard from Dolores. She ran into her at the chemist's. Now Dolores is an acquaintance of hers who's a carer. You know, she visits people's homes to help them - invalids and the like. You won't believe it, but Dolores had gone as usual to her client - she lives in one of those big Victorian villas on the side of the Hills. Oh thank you dear," and she took the cup of tea from Kylie, the young pink-haired barista, who smiled sweetly and swirled her tiny skirt - today a vivid pink scattered with large black polka dots - as she flipped her tea-towel over her shoulder and accepted Charity's money, smiling prettily as Charity waved away the prospect of change. "Where was I?"

"Dolores," prompted Emerald.

"Oh yes, Dolores. Well, when she let herself in this morning, she found her client - dead! Spread-eagled across the table. And do you know what she'd knocked to the floor when she collapsed?"

"A pot of yogurt?" ventured Tamsin.

"Oh." Charity said with disappointment, "You know?"

"I was guessing. Sorry - carry on!"

Charity sat up straighter and said. "Yes. Yogurt spilt all over the place. And a dead body."

"Did you know the victim?"

"Oh yes, didn't I say? It was Mabel Carstairs. Strange old bird. Always trying new things. As if she was searching for an answer and never quite finding it. Stomach trouble you know. She was tortured with it. But they could never find out what was wrong. I wonder if she made it all up to draw attention to herself."

"You didn't like her?" Emerald said in her usual perceptive way.

"I wouldn't go so far as to say I didn't *like* her. I've known her forever of course - she's always been in the Women's Institute, a mainstay at WI meetings, manning the tea urn. She was a decent old stick really. Dreadful thing to happen." She fondled Muffin's head, now resting on her leg. "Dolores was awfully upset, though you'd think she would be not un-used to finding dead people in her line of work."

"You say she was spread-eagled over the table and had spilt the yogurt. Perhaps it was a violent death? And Dolores is more used to her clients dying peacefully in their beds?"

"I suppose you're right, dear. Of course she was really unhappy about losing a client, though I'd have thought that was an occupational hazard. Anyway, she called an ambulance, and the ambulance people weren't satisfied and called the police. They obviously saw something in the body that worried them. Not natural, you know?"

"And the police jumped to conclusions and assumed the yogurt had poisoned Mabel Carstairs."

"My goodness, you're ahead of me, Tamsin! How did you know all this?"

And Tamsin came clean and explained their morning activities, and the connection with the tampering story in the *Malvern Mercury* which of course Charity had read with interest.

"So you see," she finished up, "it's simply not true that the yogurt could have killed her. If someone was putting a nasty taste in some pots, it certainly wasn't enough to kill anyone. It hadn't even made anyone ill - it just put them off eating any more or buying the products again. The worst thing that happened was a temporary rash from the itching powder. The idea seems to be to discredit these artisans - not to injure any customers. I don't think this death can be connected at all to the yogurt." She leant back and folded her arms.

"Hmm." Charity took a swig of her tea and gave Muffin a thoughtful stroke on the nose. "But supposing that's all a smokescreen? Supposing someone is in some way using the tampering in order to commit murder?"

"Do you mean they're making it look fairly harmless then actually killing someone so the maker of the product will get the blame?" asked Tamsin.

"Or," said Emerald quietly, "someone else is piggybacking on the doings of this nutcase to pursue their own ends."

Charity and Tamsin both turned and gazed at Emerald.

"You're right!" Tamsin exclaimed. "We've been thinking these two events are connected! But Emerald - you've seen that they may have nothing to do with each other!"

"I remember something that happened in Trotley Church - ooh, years ago now," Charity began. "There was some petty pilfering from the offertory plate. The odd florin or half-crown was going missing. The amount had dropped down quite a lot when they came to count the takings. That's how they got on to it. Those were the days when half a crown was quite a large amount." She gazed unfocussed out of the window for a moment, then snapped back to the present. "And while everyone was busy trying to find who was doing it, there was a break-in in the vestry one Sunday evening and the whole week's takings were pinched, before they could even count it."

"What's a florin?" asked Emerald, with a puzzled frown.

"Ah, my dear! You're showing my age! It was one of the old coins, like a half-crown, or a shilling - or a bob - or a thruppenny-bit, or a ten-bob note, or a guinea. Ah, those were the days, when money was straightforward!"

"You mean those days when there were twelve pennies in a shilling and twenty shillings in a pound?" laughed Tamsin, who was that bit older than Emerald and had a longer memory.

"And twenty-one shillings in a guinea. Perfectly clear!" grinned Charity. "We had to be good at maths back in those days. No calculators, you know. We'd have to work out three times six shillings and eightpence and come up with two pounds instantly."

Emerald looked baffled.

"And as for adding up five and elevenpence three-farthing and nine and fourpence ha'penny ..."

"Thank heavens for decimalisation," said Tamsin fervently, interrupting the reverie. "So what was the upshot of this thievery, Charity?"

"Oh. It turned out that the pilfering was being done by a desperate woman who had no money to feed her children. This was before the 'welfare state', of course. She'd pretend to slide a coin into the plate as it was passed round, but actually palmed a coin each time."

"And the break-in?"

"A disgruntled altar-boy. He'd been caught scrumping apples from the Vicar's garden and been reported to his parents. Children got beatings back in those days."

"The good old days when they had real money," teased Tamsin.

"I won't be provoked." Charity pulled herself up to her full 5 foot 1, then her eyes sparkled to show it was in fun. "The boy thought he'd get his own back by stealing the money and everyone would think it was the person doing the petty pilfering. But he was very young and foolish and left lots of clues, including boasting to his schoolfriends about it."

"What happened to the poor woman?" asked Emerald, always concerned for the underdog.

"The church saw their mistake in not noticing her hardship and set about organising some charity and support for her. She wasn't punished - no, no, not at all."

"And the little boy?" persisted Emerald.

"Ah, I seem to remember he was put onto heavy gardening duties in the graveyard for a while, to make amends. People kept local things local back in the day ..."

Tamsin had been quietly digesting this story, along with the last forkful of her cake. "So the small crime gave the boy the idea for the larger one. His wish to get his own back in some way. That's an interesting thought."

"But this means we're looking for two criminals!" said Emerald. "It was hard enough looking for one," she added glumly.

And the three friends all sat forlorn.

"Wondered when you'd be on the blower to me, Tamsin?" smiled Maggie down the phone later that evening after the Trotley class was finished. And they fixed to meet up in their usual orchard near Maggie's canal-side home in deepest Herefordshire.

Tamsin was looking forward to seeing her friend again, and brought Quiz, her quietest dog, who got on well with Maggie's old Labrador Jez. She'd misjudged how long it would take after her home visit - to a confused puppy that the owners couldn't understand how to housetrain - and she arrived early at the orchard. She could see the trees already covered with little green apples, some just beginning to blush with red streaks. Just as she was unloading Quiz from the back of the van, a small tractor chugged along the lane and slowed down beside her van.

"*Top Dogs!* So this is you, um - Tamsin, isn't it?"

"Hello again Jonathan. Yes. This is me."

"And you have your lovely dog with you again!"

"Quiz." Quiz looked up expectantly on hearing her name. "Yes, just Quiz today."

"I was wondering when I'd come across you here," Jonathan hopped down from the chuntering tractor and beamed at her. "Explain the *Top Dogs* thing to me."

"Ah, that's my dog school," said Tamsin with pride. "I train dogs - all force-free and dog-friendly," she added quickly, always keen that people didn't start talking about the importance of showing the dog who's boss.

But Jonathan said, "I have a mutt at home who could do with your ministrations. Perhaps you should come round some time?"

"What sort of 'mutt'?"

"Actually, he's not a mutt at all. He's a pure-bred working English Springer Spaniel. Very expensive. I got him when I thought I'd do more shooting."

"And do you shoot over him now?" asked Tamsin tentatively, picking up the past tense in his statement. She'd never got used to how people could enjoy killing birds for sport. For the pot, maybe. But for fun?

So she was relieved to hear Jonathan saying, "No. I hadn't had him long when I winged a bird and I was really upset about it. And Teal turned out to be afraid of gunshot anyway, so perhaps it was meant."

"I'm glad you don't shoot any more," she said quietly.

"And then I started the business, so there's little time for that even if I wanted to. But Teal's afraid of lots of things. Do you help with that? To make his life easier?"

"Definitely! I love helping dogs gain confidence." And before she knew it she had a visit to *The Cider Flagon* booked into her calendar.

"Um .." He spoke hesitantly. "You know all that hoohah at the market last week?" Tamsin nodded encouragingly as she slipped her phone back into her pocket. "It's awful that someone's targeting these makers. They're just honest folk trying to turn an honest penny - not big business. Anyway - I thought I'd better check my stock when I got back on Saturday night .." He paused. Tamsin looked up at him. "Know what I found?"

Tamsin waited.

"There were tiny needle marks in the foil - you know, the wrappers round the corks. They need to be champagne-style corks, and the black and gold wrappers look swish. So I investigated further and found something had been injected through the cork. I opened the bottle and tasted it - it was metallic and bitter!"

"No!"

"So I checked all the bottles I had there. There were three with needle marks, and they'd all been in a crate just under the table. Someone must have bent down and lifted the side flap of the stand and done it."

"That's awful! What did you do with the bottles?"

"Chucked them. Tipped my lovely cider down the drain," he sighed.

"I suppose it could have been done without anyone noticing. You could bend down to tie your shoelace, or sort through your shopping bag .."

"Or pet your dog!" He raised his eyebrows then smiled showing he was just teasing. "You're right - I never saw them, and it would be easy enough to do. I'm only glad I didn't sell any from that crate."

"Too right! But it's not just the artisans at the market, you know. Others have been affected. People who supply to small independent shops, you know? Then, of course, the shopkeepers get it in the neck."

"Clearly some sort of nut .. The question is, how are we going to stop it?"

Tamsin felt flattered that she was included in the 'we'. "I think things may start moving pretty soon. Have you heard about the old lady in Malvern?"

Jonathan shook his head. "Malvern has many old ladies. What about this one?"

"She died, and there's some suggestion that there was a poisoned product at the scene. So the police are now involved - in that part, at least."

"So someone's actually died from this nonsense?" Jonathan looked suitably appalled.

"Well, I haven't heard what she actually died of. Maybe it was coincidence. They're doing a PM, of course."

Jonathan tapped the side of his nose and nodded. "And you just happen to be taking a walk with our friendly local police pathologist .."

Tamsin scuffed her boot on the stones. "Well, we've done this sort of thing before .."

"Gottit! Now I can place you! That man who died at a dog class - that was you!"

"And the Robin Hood wannabe down the road from here," she smiled.

"And weren't you mixed up in that horse-racing thing?"

Tamsin beamed proudly, "and the bike-racing!"

"Ah well, we're in good hands! Clearly no Malvern malefactors are safe!" he laughed. "And if I'm not mistaken, here's your walking companion." They both turned to see Maggie's sleek black car trundling along the lane. "I'll leave you to it. And I'll see you next Thursday. You can tell me all about it then." And he hopped up into his tractor and waved cheerily to Maggie as he pulled away to give her space to park.

So when Maggie got Jez out of the car, returning Jonathan's greeting, and came and joined her and Quiz, Tamsin was feeling pretty pleased with herself.

CHAPTER TWELVE

"Ho there, Tamsin!" called Maggie as she led Jez over to the entrance to the orchard. "Go and have a mooch with Quiz," she said loudly to her old and slightly deaf black lab as she released him.

The two dogs ambled forward, glad of the shade of the apple trees, happily hoovering up all the summer scents with their amazing noses.

Maggie adjusted her floppy sun-hat and waved her hands to encompass the orchard and the sky. "Isn't this beautiful!" as she gave Tamsin a welcoming hug. "Funny," she went on, smiling at her friend, "how we always seem to meet up for a walk when dastardly deeds have been done?"

"That is funny, yes," replied Tamsin with a sweet smile. "Dastardly deeds are an occupational hazard for you, I dare say. But they keep landing on my plate too."

"So how is the death of a lonely old woman landing on your plate?"

"Yogurt."

Maggie looked perplexed.

"It's the goats' yogurt she'd been eating recently. That connects it with the contamination being inflicted on a number of the local artisans."

"Contamination? I hadn't heard about that."

"Aha, you don't read the *Malvern Mercury!* Yeah. Someone's been tampering with the craft makers' products. Itching powder in the knitting, metallic taste in the yogurt, funny-tasting scones, and Jonathan was just saying some of his cider has been interfered with ..."

"How awful! Those folk work so hard to follow their passion and produce beautiful things. I've got some really good food from the local makers. Who on earth would do a thing like that?"

"Some nut, I suppose, or someone with a grudge .." Tamsin stopped mid-stride and gazed into the middle distance. "I wonder .."

"Run the malefactor to ground already, Tamsin?"

"I was just thinking of someone who's disgruntled, someone involved with these makers. But you know, so far nothing dangerous has been put in the products. Nothing that would *kill* anyone."

"And you want to know if someone's upped the ante and poisoned Mabel Carstairs?"

"Exactly," grinned Tamsin broadly, as she scooped up a fallen apple and tossed it into the long grass at the edge of the orchard for Quiz and Jez to hunt for.

"The short answer is yes. She was murdered. And yes, she was poisoned. Where the poison came from is something SOCO and the forensics guys are hunting her house for now."

"Goodness! Fancy your home becoming a 'Scene of Crime'." Tamsin shuddered. "What was the poison? Did it have a metallic taste?"

"It was thallium, so no, no taste. That's why it's a popular pesticide. No smell, no taste. The little critters munch their way through the bait without a care in the world."

"Till they thud on to their backs, stiff."

"Not exactly. It tends to accumulate in the body - but fairly fast. So the rats may gradually get sicker. It's commonly used for vermin in the Middle East."

"But not here? I have to say, I'd never heard of it."

"Not here. It's illegal for general sale here. Though it is used in some production processes - electronics, glass lenses, and fibre optics, I know - probably others too."

"So whoever did it has some science connection?"

"Maybe."

Tamsin thought for a while as she went to see what Quiz was rootling through the dry grass for. "All sorted, Quiz? A mouse perhaps?" Then she turned back to Maggie and said, "Did she have any relatives? Anyone shown up to claim their inheritance?"

"It seems there's a nephew. They're trying to get hold of him. We haven't got an official identification yet."

"I wonder ... I could see if I could have a chat with the carer - the one who found her. She must know something. And if thallium is a slow burn, then Mabel should have been showing symptoms already."

"I suppose there's no point in me suggesting you leave this to the police?"

"None whatever!" Tamsin turned to grin at Maggie. "There's something going on with all these makers being messed about. And I want to get it stopped. I wonder whether there's a nut doing that in order to shift the blame for the murder he wanted to commit ..."

"He or she," corrected Maggie quietly.

"He or she - quite so. Or whether someone else is piggybacking on the contaminations for their own ends. I'm willing to bet that if your forensics guys find anything other than possibly a metallic taste in the yogurt pots, then it was put there by someone in the house."

"If they were putting deadly poison into yogurt in the shops, then Mabel Carstairs would not be the only victim," Maggie nodded slowly.

"Exactly. Here Quiz!" and she gave her dog a treat, just because, and then one to Jez who came plodding after her, gazing with his slightly cloudy old eyes.

"But the poison could have been in anything. It can even be absorbed through the skin, so they're bringing us in samples of the soap, clothes - all sorts."

"Really?" Tamsin looked up quickly from giving the dogs dreamy smiles.

"Yep. So, how are you going to track down this carer without crossing Chief Inspector Hawkins?"

"Don't forget I have my own secret weapon ..."

"Charity?"

"Charity! I'll put money on her knowing everything there is to know about this person, and certainly knowing how to find her fast. She has a fleet of old ladies who keep their ears and eyes open, and regularly compare notes over tea and Bath Buns. I stayed in the home of one of them when I first arrived in Malvern - after the explorer job."

"I forgot you have such a diverse past!"

Tamsin grinned, her dimples making one of their occasional appearances. "I needed a place to live and Charity got me sorted in one phone call. So yes, if Charity doesn't know, Dorothy's bound to. I'll head over there before my next client."

They'd completed two circuits of the orchard - keeping cool in the shade of the apple-laden trees - and as Tamsin collected Quiz to go to the van she added, "I wouldn't be surprised if between Charity and Dorothy they know all there is to know about the Carstairs family as well. Perhaps they'll know how to find the nephew."

"Happy hunting!"

"Oh - when will you know about what Forensics find?"

"That's not exactly going to be public knowledge, unless Hawkins decides to release it," Maggie wagged a finger.

"I'm hardly 'public'!" laughed Tamsin as Quiz hopped into the back of the *Top Dogs* van. And the two friends departed, Maggie back to chopping up bodies in the mortuary, and Tamsin to grill Dorothy then on to Ledbury to help persuade a noisy dog that just because he was a Pomeranian didn't mean he had to bark all the time.

CHAPTER THIRTEEN

"Tamsin, my dear!" exclaimed Dorothy when she opened her front door, "How wonderful to see you! And how's your lovely Quiz?" Instead of her usual cardigan and tweed skirt, Dorothy was wearing a quaint summer dress, full-skirted and with a floral pattern, that Tamsin thought probably dated from her girlhood in the 50s.

"You look lovely, Dorothy! So summery." Dorothy blushed sweetly. "She's here in the van - would you like to see her?"

"Oh, bring her in! Bring her in! She was such an enchanting puppy."

So Tamsin released Quiz from the van, who spotted her old friend Dorothy and scampered down the path and nuzzled her.

"She still has just the one ear up and one down," smiled Dorothy fondly. "I remember that's why you called her Quiz."

"She's a treasure! And I'm so glad you were happy to let me get a puppy when I was living with you."

"So am I! And look what's come of it, you and your wonderful dog school." By now they'd reached the kitchen and Quiz met up with another old friend, Dorothy's dog who used to steal food and got lessons in lieu of some of Tamsin's rent. "Eddie is pretty old now, doesn't hear so well."

"But he's a happy fellow, aren't you Eddie?" Tamsin said, raising her voice to address the small dog, who responded to the visitors with a happy tail-wag.

"And of course I have to thank you Tamsin, for introducing me to the idea of having a B&B and giving myself an income in my dotage, as well as an interest," said Dorothy as she started assembling tea-things.

"You're a natch! Here, let me - I can still remember where everything is." And Tamsin filled the kettle and reached for the teapot while Dorothy opened an old Christmas-themed tin with her slightly shaky hands and found some treats for both dogs.

When they eventually fetched up in the living room, with tea in the best china tea service, and Madeira cake with little forks, Dorothy said, "Charity tells me you're on the warpath again, dear - campaigning for the artisan underdogs?"

"I am. I can't help myself. You know I hate to see injustice. That's probably why I work to change people's attitude to their dogs - I hate to see how they\re misunderstood. And I'm hoping you may be able to help me."

"I don't have anything to add about the funny-tasting cakes. I just heard about it when I was chatting to Linda in *Health in the Hills* the other day."

"I think we have plenty of information about that. What I'm wondering is ... who is the carer for the lady who died yesterday?"

"Mabel Carstairs? Oh, wasn't that shocking! She was *years* younger than me. Always a bit of a fusspot about her health, but," she leant forward in her armchair, "I never thought there was much wrong with her."

"And yet she needed a carer?"

"Not sure she *needed* her - but she liked to feel important. And she could afford to pay. Oh, I know one shouldn't speak ill of the dead .."

"Why not? Seems to me the best time to speak ill of someone, when they can't fight back," grinned Tamsin.

"Now I know you don't really mean that," Dorothy laughed in reply.

"So - who is the carer? You see, I'd like to have a chat with her - find out if Mabel was sickening before she died."

"It's Dolores Baxter. I know her through the Women's Institute."

"The good ole WI!"

"She's been doing this kind of work for years, ever since her husband left for that floozie who used to work in the Goat and Compasses. Well, I'm not sure he left for her - he always had a roving eye, and she's the last one I actually knew about before he disappeared." Dorothy took a sip of tea. "Dolores is fairly good at the work, I'd guess. Will I give you an introduction? I can ring her now."

"Oh, that would be marvellous! Yes please."

"Let me find the number .. and while I'm doing that you can explain to me exactly why you want to know all this."

Tamsin explained the connection between the death and the yogurt pots, Susannah's precarious position and the full extent so far of the contamination scare.

"It's getting serious. I see now. You have to pursue this, Tamsin! Those poor makers .."

So a date was fixed for Tamsin to visit Dolores the next day before her Friday afternoon puppy class. And as she settled back in her armchair and enjoyed another slice of Madeira cake, Dorothy, eyes a-sparkle, said, "I wonder your detective nose isn't twitching, Tamsin dear."

"Oh?"

"You see, as well as knowing Mabel for years - always a busy person, never married, active in all the charitable organisations and so on - I also knew her brother."

Tamsin gasped, "So you know her nephew?"

"I not only know him, but when he pays his duty calls to his aunt, he always stays here, right in my little B&B! He was here only last week ..."

"You are a marvel, Dorothy. Go on, hand over the details!"

And so when Tamsin left her old friend, she was armed with an appointment with the carer, Dolores, and the mobile number for nephew Reggie Carstairs, and furthermore she was full of cake.

"This detecting business is a doddle," she said to Quiz as they climbed back into the van, "if you know who to ask!"

CHAPTER FOURTEEN

Tamsin didn't know what Reggie did for a living, but felt it was a safe bet to ring him around lunchtime. And she got him when he appeared to be striding along a busy pavement in a town, puffing slightly - whether from being unfit, or the heat, or because he was in a hurry to get his lunch she didn't know. But he accepted her call as she shamelessly used Dorothy's name to introduce herself, and offered her condolences - being sure not to speak any ill!

"Thank you. But I'm not unduly upset. She was a creaking gate, you know? I was at Dorothy's last week, came up to visit Aunt Mabel."

"Just last week? Ooh, did you notice anything about your aunt? Anything unusual?"

"Nope. She was the same as ever. She always had a bee in her bonnet about her health, though she was actually as strong as an ox and should have gone on for donkey's years. I work in a research lab in Cambridge and have to visit the Science Park in Malvern from time to time, so I visit the old aunt at the same time."

A scientist! Tamsin's ears pricked up. "Oh, the Science Park!"

"Hot spot for inventions, nestled there in the sleepy Malvern Hills."

"Fascinating! Lots of eggheads in Malvern," she laughed. "And you're involved in that kind of work?"

" 'Fraid what I do is classified. But broadly speaking, yes. Anyway, what's your interest in Auntie Mabel?" He seemed to have stopped walking to wait for traffic to pass and was paying more attention to the conversation.

"Well, it seems that there may be some connection between her unfortunate death and the recent outbreak of contamination of artisan food makers' products."

"You mean one of these hippies killed my aunt?" He raised his voice over the roar of traffic.

"No no, not at all. Someone has been sabotaging their products. And the police are investigating. I have a lot of friends in the creator community, so when Dorothy told me you visited her regularly, I thought I'd ask you. You see, some madman has been putting nasty-tasting stuff in their products, so people stop buying them. Nothing that would actually kill anyone." She realised she was talking too much. "I believe your aunt was into health foods?"

"Oh yes, the place was stuffed with them. All sorts of supplements and strange foods. Look, I didn't really take much interest in her. A short visit was enough - annoying old bat really. Father's sister. Duty, you know? I just would visit when I was over her way. And before you ask, I had no expectations. For all I know she left everything to the cats' home. My skills are well-rewarded already. *Tax-iii!*" he shouted loudly, so that Tamsin almost dropped the phone and all three dogs looked up from their beds. "Gotta go now, ok?"

"Of course, thanks for your help."

"Help?"

"Yes! Thank you. Will you be over for the funeral?"

"Marble Arch!" he said to the taxi-driver and to Tamsin, "I suppose so. Don't even know when they're releasing her body. They only told me this morning. Gotta go." And the line went dead.

Tamsin tapped the phone to her mouth as she digested what she'd just heard. "He was a bit quick to deny an interest in her will," she said to the dogs, who could make no sense of what she was saying and lost interest as she didn't appear to be asking them to do anything where a treat may be on offer. "And that big house must be worth a good figure."

So when she arrived at Dolores Baxter's scruffy little house in Malvern Link after lunch, she had a load of questions to ask her. The carer was plump and Spanish in appearance with a slight Spanish accent, and her living quarters were dull and drab and smelt strongly of cat. While she didn't appear to be living in poverty, there was equally no sign of abundance in her home. The kitchen lino was worn pale, scuffed and buckled. Everything appeared second-hand, tawdry, past it.

"So you're a friend of Dorothy's?" Dolores asked suspiciously as she parked Tamsin in the poky kitchen at the little round table covered with a slightly sticky oilcloth. She hastily removed the remains of a takeaway meal, dumping it all in the sink, and two cats instantly started winding themselves round their visitor's legs.

"Hello Pusscats ... Yes! I've known her ever since I arrived in Malvern. You're a blow-in too, I'll hazard a guess?"

"I am." Dolores gazed at a big vibrant picture on the wall, of a sun-drenched beach, with brightly-coloured umbrellas shielding the jolly holidaymakers from some of the sun. The vivid blue sea looked very enticing to Tamsin in the sweltering heatwave they were enduring. "But I married an Englishman, so I fetched up here." She turned back to Tamsin, a fixed smile on her face.

"And you decided to stay."

"I'd started care work before my husband ran off. Then when he left me I needed to get away, so I went out to the Middle East for a while, looking after people in their homes. Thought there'd be plenty of money there. But they don't get rich by giving their money away, as my mother used to say. I couldn't get used to the culture there so I came back and joined an agency here. Bit of a come-down, really," she sighed. "Being a skivvy for people who have enough money to be able to have a servant."

"I thought you were a carer - don't you look after sick people?"

Tamsin smiled encouragingly, thinking how well Dolores had adapted to English, with barely any noticeable accent.

"I do, yes. Mostly," she smiled back, genuinely this time. "And some of them are alright, I suppose. I cook meals for them as well. I certainly don't do it for the money." She snorted as she gazed at the sunny image on the wall again, then turned back to Tamsin. "And you want to know about Miss Carstairs?"

"I do. Tell me, how long did you work for her?"

Dolores gazed at the sunny picture and said, "Three years. Quite a while. Quite often it's only a short time I'm with someone." A cold look came into her eye as she turned back to Tamsin, "Natural wastage, you know?"

Tamsin gulped silently. "And Miss Carstairs, had she been sickening recently, feeling unwell, acting odd?"

Dolores leant forward, elbows on the table, "Now you come to mention it, she had. Not that I thought she was at death's door. She always liked to put on an act - 'I'm a martyr to my health,' she'd say - but she was pretty tough."

"So what made you think she was genuinely unwell?"

"A number of things, now I look back at it. I've been thinking about it, so I remembered things I didn't really notice at the time. Very odd - when I did her hair for her, I had to clean a lot of hair off the brush afterwards. She had thick hair so she wasn't looking bald, but she was definitely losing hair. I didn't say anything, of course. Then she complained of having a tummy bug - though it didn't seem to affect her appetite! All that yogurt and stone-baked brown bread she was wolfing down, yogurt was her latest thing and it had to be goats' yogurt. And you know, it is hot at the moment, but she kept complaining that her feet were burning. She'd walk about barefoot on the kitchen tiles to cool them down. Weird."

"A strange collection of symptoms," agreed Tamsin, mentally ticking them off the list of symptoms for thallium poisoning that she'd looked up on the web after talking to Maggie. "So you didn't feel she was seriously ill?"

"No. Not at that stage. But the day before she died she started rambling. Confused, you know? I thought maybe she was getting dementia - so many of my clients have it. When I arrived and found her dead at the kitchen table, arms spread out, yogurt pot knocked over, yogurt everywhere, I was bothered by it. It just didn't seem normal - I'm used to old people dying, you see."

"I guess you are," nodded Tamsin, absently stroking the cat that had materialised on her lap.

"So when the ambulance arrived they thought it seemed a bit odd too. That's why the police got involved."

"And have you heard what she actually died from?" asked Tamsin tentatively.

"No. Not heard anything. But I would like to know, some time. I wonder if I should have noticed more, you know?"

"Did it surprise you that the police are taking such an interest? Going over the house in their SOCO suits?"

"Well," Dolores leant forward again, looking round as if someone may be overhearing, and said, "That nephew." She shut her mouth firmly and sat back in her chair again, and carried on stroking the second cat which had found its way onto her lap.

"That nephew?"

"Yes. Reggie his name is. He'd drop in to visit now and again. He clearly didn't like Miss Carstairs very much, and left as soon as he'd had some tea. I wonder .."

"Yes?" encouraged Tamsin.

"I wonder if he was keeping in with her in the hope of getting something in her will. That house is worth a small fortune." She clamped her lips shut again.

"And you think he may have been anxious to get his inheritance sooner rather than later?" Tamsin asked quietly.

"Oh, I wouldn't say that!" said Dolores, having implied exactly that. "Just saying, that's all." And she stroked the cat more vigorously.

Tamsin didn't feel she would learn much more on this visit, so after a bit of chat about the cats and hearing more about the provenance of the beach picture - that it came from the seaside village Dolores had been brought up in - she wound up the conversation on a friendly note. 'Need to keep this line of communication open!' She thought to herself as she climbed back into the Top Dogs van and set off for the pure joy of her Puppy Class. It was one of the high points of her week: six puppies with big round eyes and open souls, and six or more owners who were doing their best to accommodate this new person in their lives.

CHAPTER FIFTEEN

Tamsin was used to visiting people in their homes in the course of her work. But people usually made an effort to at least tidy up a bit before she came. After the fusty drabness of Dolores's house, Tamsin wanted some colour and luxury, so she assembled the troops and she and Emerald, accompanied by all three dogs, met Feargal at The Cake Stop the next morning.

As usual, Feargal raced in from the blazing sunshine outside as if he had a train to catch, and ordered a massive amount of food to eat along with his coffee. "Morning Jean-Philippe! Morning Kylie!" He seemed full of the joys of spring as he busied himself fitting all his purchases onto the round table between the armchairs that Tamsin had drawn up for them.

"Slow down!" said Emerald, "You're making me feel hot!"

"Give it a minute and you'll be complaining that the air conditioning is too cold!" said Feargal as he took a huge bite out of his toasted Panini, cheese dripping out of it onto his plate. Moonbeam, who was sitting on Tamsin's lap, watched the falling drips and crumbs with rapt attention, and would have been on the floor in a trice had any missed the plate.

While he made short work of his meal Emerald said, "It was so hot in the upper room for my last yoga class that I had to open the fire escape door."

"Oh." Tamsin said meaningfully.

"Yeah it was the first time since - well you know when - and it felt pretty weird."

"Why don't you buy a fan instead, then you won't have to open that door?"

"That's exactly what I'm going to do today. No more dark memories."

The two women waited patiently while Feargal scoffed his food. They knew well enough that until the beast was fed they'd get no sense out of him. And, as he ate at huge speed, they didn't have to wait long.

"Ok," he said, swiping his hands to remove all the crumbs, and holding his fingers out to Banjo to lick the cheesy remains off them. Tamsin was pleased to see her shy dog getting braver with people he knew. "What's the latest?"

"I suppose there's no point in wondering if you know about Mabel Carstairs' death?"

"None at all," grinned Feargal, tossing his auburn curls back off his forehead.

"And the yogurt connection?"

"Yep. No point."

"Ok," she smiled. "I wanted to know more about what's going on here. So first of all I rang the nephew, one Reggie Carstairs. Turns out he's a *scientist!*" she said with emphasis. "And out of the blue he announced that he had no interest in Mabel's will."

"Now why would he do that?" asked Feargal, stroking his chin. "'The lady doth protest too much, methinks' ..."

"Never expected to hear you quoting Hamlet!" Emerald murmured as she looked admiringly at the bundle of energy that was Feargal.

"Why indeed!" retorted Tamsin. "I hadn't mentioned it at all. Apparently he would visit his aunt when he had to work at the Science Park."

"The Science Park? That big place at the bottom of the Common? Isn't that where they developed radar?" asked Emerald.

"Yeah, and infra-red imaging I believe," added Tamsin.

"They did," Feargal chipped in. "I did a piece on the place not so long ago, so some of the info is still lurking in my mind. Used to be a government facility in the War. Espionage and counter-espionage, you know? Then they carried on after, inventing away."

"What else did they invent?" asked Emerald.

"Um," Feargal thought hard, "they invented the first touch screen - sixty years ago - long before smartphones and tablets were even thought of. They developed it for air traffic control. Then there's thermal imaging," he counted the items off on his fingers, "laser technology, drones, radar-blocking, even microwaves - you name it." He ran out of fingers and waved all of them in the air.

"Wow, all that in little old Malvern!"

"There's more, now I come to think of it. There's satnav, stealth materials to conceal drones and wind farms, weather forecasting, special scientific lenses - they're a hive of activity, the place is literally bristling with brains."

"Can you visit it?" asked Emerald, who sometimes didn't seem to dwell on this planet very often.

"No! It's all very hush-hush. You have to sign the Official Secrets Act to work there. All this counter-espionage sort of stuff they do. After all, their work on radar played a large part in winning the last war. You wouldn't want that kind of info getting out!"

Emerald, for whom the last war was a distant none-too-tasteful event that her grandparents talked about, looked slightly chastened, but nodded all the same.

"So I wonder what Reggie does? He said it was classified. He works in a research lab in Cambridge, he said."

"Cambridge is another hotbed of inventions - specially tech ones. If you can get me the name of his lab I may be able to find out more. Do you think he's involved in all this?"

"Not really, I have to say." Tamsin sounded disappointed at losing a possible suspect. "Obviously he'd find it easy enough to contaminate the products - he'd have access to stuff. But surely that can't be laid at his door?"

"Doubt it. He wouldn't know the market people. And presumably he only visits occasionally. But this thallium that Mabel died from - you can't get it in England - I've been researching. But it *is* used in some manufacturing processes, notably for lenses," Feargal raised an eyebrow. "I wonder ..."

"If he wanted to bump her off, he surely wouldn't use an exotic chemical that could only be got by .. people like him?" Emerald objected, most reasonably.

"He's got to be brainy. And you're absolutely right, Em, that would not be brainy." Tamsin studied the inside of her empty coffee cup for a moment, debating whether to have another. But instead she said, "And I'll tell you about my second bit of investigating for the day - and it was someone who definitely isn't over-brainy."

They looked expectantly at her.

"I visited Dolores Baxter."

"Mabel's carer!" said Feargal, who clearly knew an awful lot about the case.

"The same. She's disgruntled. Somewhat resentful. Thinks she's come down the social ladder, doing what she does. She's obviously short of money. She noticed a number of symptoms in Mabel over the week or so before she died, that all point to thallium poisoning. Everything she mentioned is on the list I found of symptoms and side-effects."

Emerald gasped, "So she'd been steadily poisoned over a period of time?"

"That's apparently the way to do it. What symptoms did Dolores see?" asked Feargal.

"Hair loss, tummy trouble, um, burning sensation in the feet, oh, and confusion. And yes, Emerald, it apparently takes a little while to build up in the body."

Emerald shivered. "Nasty." And she invited Moonbeam over onto her lap so she could have a soothing cuddle.

"Very nasty. And not related to the types of contamination of the products, which are unpleasant but so far not dangerous. Anyhow,

Dolores had worked for Mabel for some time, and maybe she made herself indispensable."

"She was expecting to be left something, you mean?" asked Emerald, twirling Moonbeam's ears as the little dog lay on her lap, her eyes closed, a blissful expression on her face.

"Maybe. Oh, and hear this! She used to work in the Middle East. That's where thallium is readily available apparently, for pests."

"Won't the police be questioning her?" Emerald asked.

"You would imagine so. And I guess a look at Mabel's will wouldn't go amiss."

"So that's two people who may think they could expect something when she died. And both of them had the ability to get hold of this deadly poison." Feargal waved to Kylie over at the counter and pointed to the coffee cups on the table. Kylie gave a thumbs-up and got to work brewing. She knew well what each of them liked.

"It's a bit thin. But why else would anyone murder her?" Tamsin spread her hands out and shrugged. "Charity said she was a decent old stick and a mainstay of the WI tea counter."

"It's a puzzle alright. We've been running this campaign at the *Mercury* for a few days now. Lots of cranks and nuts coming out with ideas and conspiracy theories and all the rest. But three people have actually pointed the finger at the same possible malefactor."

"Oh really! Who?"

"The reports were anonymous, so we can't give them too much credence. Could be the same person saying it three times, in fact. They point to a man called John Curtin."

"Curtin? That was the man who was kicking up a fuss at the market! He was upset because he hadn't been offered a stall. What does he do, I wonder?"

"I remembered you telling me about him. So I did a bit of 'investigative journalism'," Feargal grinned. "He wants to make some sort of metal-work ornaments."

"Then why was he trying to get in the food market?"

"They do have *Sheep's Clothing*," Emerald pointed out. "Maybe he wants to make plates or dishes or something that would fit there."

"Oh, maybe he was trying to get into the Craft Market - that's run by the same people."

"Well, there's more to him than that." Feargal paused for effect. "He used to work at the Science Park. Till he got the sack."

"Ohhh!" exclaimed Tamsin. "Another scientist! And he may have had access to thallium, or just knew what was harmless but nasty-tasting."

"I know what he'd use!" Emerald jumped forward, almost ejecting Moonbeam on to the floor. "Essence of Brussels sprouts!"

That was the moment Kylie arrived with the fresh coffees. "Well, you're having a high ole time," she said, as they all rocked with laughter and Feargal wafted his card over her little machine, being careful to pocket the receipt for expenses.

And it did lighten the mood enough for them to enjoy their coffee and leave the thorny subject of whodunit and whydunit for a while, having shared out their tasks for the next day: Feargal to carry on investigating the science lead, and Tamsin to talk to some of the market people and find out more about John Curtin.

"I could make a start on that tomorrow, maybe."

"Oh, I nearly forgot!" Emerald put her hand over her mouth. "Susannah rang today. She's still so frantic and worried. I promised we'd go over there tomorrow to play with the kids again - I mean, *help* with the goats."

"I'll love that! Poor Susannah. We'll be able to reassure her slightly, given what we've learned. And she may know something about this Curtin geezer. I'll look forward to that. Goats are such characters, and they seem to relish this hot sun. We can play in the meadow with them!"

"Do you think this hot weather will ever end?" said Feargal, picking up on the British love of discussing the weather.

"Who knows? We'll be complaining enough when the summer is over, so I guess we have to put up with it," replied Tamsin in her matter-of-fact way. "I have to say it's very beautiful up on the Hills late at night.

That's when we do some of our Search & Rescue training. It's blissfully cool but there's still warmth in the ground. Perfect!"

"Ah yes, you were inspired by the mountain bike affair to start that, weren't you. Banjo is the chosen one, am I right?" asked Feargal.

"Banjo is doing great, aren't you, Banjo Bunny?" Tamsin fondled her pretty grey dog's mane as he gazed up at her at the mention of his name. "It suits him down to the ground, as he doesn't have to deal with strange people or other dogs. There are other dogs in the team, of course, but they all work individually."

"Wouldn't want to have dogs fighting over you if you were being rescued ..."

"We're actually doing work on finding dead bodies right now, so that wouldn't be an issue," she grinned.

"But if they're using their noses, how do you practice?" puzzled Emerald.

"You can buy cadaver scent. In a bottle."

"E-uuuu," Emerald shuddered.

"Sure can!" laughed Feargal, "*Eau de Mort* - it's my perfume of choice when I'm going out for the evening. Particularly good for attracting ghouls and vampires."

And when Jean-Philippe came over to greet them, they were all helpless with laughter again.

CHAPTER SIXTEEN

"Really, it's hard to be anything but happy when you've got these kids to play with!" Emerald laughed, as she watched a kid scramble up onto a barrel lying on its side in the little paddock, and dance and cavort, leaping and twisting in mid-air. Another hopped up and they played "King of the castle" as one slithered off and another joined in the game.

"It's amazing how sure-footed they are - with hooves instead of paws," said Tamsin as she watched them.

"They are a delight - and you should see them leapin' about on the side of a craggy mountain!" agreed Susannah who, since her friends had come to help her that morning - whizzing through the chores in jig time - had lost some of the furrows in her brow. Her shoulders were relaxing and she was laughing for the first time in days.

It was a glorious summer's day, the white goats sparkling in the sunshine, the coats of the coloured goats shining glossily. Some of them were lying down cudding rapidly, swallowing the chewed food then bringing up the next parcel of food.

"Ooh, you can see it go up their neck!" said Emerald, fascinated. "What are they re-chewing?"

"Chewing for the first time really. When they browse they take in as much vegetation as they can, then sort it out later. See those stinging nettles lying over by the hedge, where the hens are pecking? They love those and some will eat them growing, but most goats prefer them cut and wilted."

Emerald wrinkled her nose at the thought of chewing stinging nettles. "How does their body know to send up un-chewed food?"

"Ah! They have four stomachs," explained Susannah. "The biggest is the rumen, where the food is coming up from to be cudded." She tickled a kid fondly behind the ear. "That's where we get our word 'ruminating'."

"Ah, I get it! Chewing things over!" Emerald laughed.

"I wish I had four stomachs," said Tamsin brightly, patting her tummy, "Two of them would be devoted to cake!"

"Speaking of which," laughed Susannah, looking so much better, "I've never got this far ahead so early - let's go inside. I've made a treat to go with your coffee."

"I'm always up for a treat!" said Tamsin as she stroked the quietest of the kids who was leaning against her.

"Come on then, slowcoach!" and Emerald trotted ahead after Susannah.

"But how do you get time to make treats?" Tamsin, having torn herself away from the enchanting kid, caught up with them as they walked into the house together.

"You were so helpful last time you visited - I had to do something for you. And," she shifted the kettle onto the hotplate of her Aga, "I didn't have any yogurt to pack. Orders are down. So the kids are getting the extra milk, and the billies and the hens love it too. Do sit down!"

Tamsin and Emerald exchanged sighing glances. "I know that look," said Emerald quietly, as she detected the steely determination in her friend's eye. Tamsin, nicknamed The Malvern Hills Detective, was on the rampage for justice once more.

The special treat was a beautiful sponge cake with goats' cream, and strawberries from Susannah's little garden.

"Mmm, this is just delicious! I'd never have known it was goats' cream," said Emerald, polishing off her plateful.

"People seem to think that goats' products should taste 'goaty' and nasty. But if you treat the milk carefully and keep the billies right away from the dairy - and of course feed the goats right - then it's sweet and delicious."

"It certainly is," said Tamsin appreciatively, eagerly accepting the offer of second helpings. "And the cake is such a lovely colour!"

"That's real free range eggs for you! Come on Emerald, I can't eat all the rest of this by myself, and it needs eating today!"

Emerald caved in and enjoyed another slice of the cake. "I'm glad to see you looking a bit happier, Susannah. It must have been a really hard time for you recently."

"It's been *awful!* Nobody's telling me anything, so I don't know whether the police still think I killed that poor woman."

"They haven't arrested you? Or taken you in for questioning?" Tamsin paused while bringing a forkful of goodness up to her mouth.

"They haven't. Nothing since that first day."

"Then surely they can't think it was anything to do with you! You can be certain they'd have you under lock and key already if they had anything on you."

"That's one way of looking at it, I suppose. But I wish I knew."

"Of course. The last I heard they're testing everything in Mabel's house to locate the poison. My guess is that if they'd found it in your yogurt pots they'd be taking your place apart by now."

Susannah sighed and put her head in her hands at the very thought of that.

"Hey, have you found any more contaminated pots?"

"No. And I'm being ultra-cautious now. I only do the Farmers' Market occasionally, when I have more than I can shift quickly, and when I next go I'll be sure to keep everything away from the front of the stand. I have to keep it in the fridge unit anyway in this boiling weather! I checked over all the yogurt I had which was date-stamped before the Open Day. I discarded any with pin-pricks of course, and fed all the clean stuff to the hens and the kids. And I'm putting an extra paper wrapper round the pots that go to shops, *and* I've told the shopkeepers to quickly check the pot before handing it over to a customer. Pin-pricks will show up clearly on paper."

"What a clever idea!" Emerald said admiringly.

"You're doing everything you can," nodded Tamsin. "Say, have you all any ideas about who's doing this? You artisans must all be talking to each other!"

"We sure are. And although nobody actually knows anything, there's one person whose name keeps coming up."

Tamsin raised her eyebrows expectantly.

"It's John Curtin."

"John Curtin. Now he was the bloke who was kicking up about being passed over for a stand. Not a very pleasant person, it seems."

"Do you know him?" asked Emerald.

"No, I've never seen him. I heard he was there once, complaining bitterly to poor Felicity. She's a good old soul and runs the market well, I think. He was borderline rude to her, implying it was her fault he was rejected and that she must have something personal against him."

"Hey!" Tamsin jumped in. "You've never seen him? But perhaps you have! Perhaps he was at your Open Day?"

"Oh my God! Perhaps he was! I wouldn't have known. There was a great crowd, families, children .. I've been going over and over in my mind who was there."

"That could be it then. And it seems he keeps going back to the market to complain. He can't accept his fate. It would fit - that he's blaming everyone else for his own shortcomings, so he wants to get back at them."

"And wasn't he thrown out of the Science Park?" prompted Emerald.

"Yes! I nearly forgot. We don't know why he was, but he'd have all the know-how to do .. either of these awful things."

"Or both?" asked Susannah, looking perkier at the revelation that Tamsin and Emerald were clearly doing some investigating.

"That's a good question! We started off thinking that it was the same perpetrator for both things/"

"*Perp!*" giggled Emerald. "Get the lingo!"

"Perp, if you insist," grinned Tamsin, wrinkling her nose with distaste at the inelegant word. "Then we kinda thought it was more likely someone was taking the opportunity of the contaminations to do a bit of their own dirty work."

"Or, you know," Emerald said slowly, "they could be totally unconnected. Someone who didn't know about the artisans' problem - just decided to bump off Miss Carstairs."

"Someone not from this area, you're thinking?"

"Or someone not in touch with healthy eating and good living .."

"Reggie and Dolores." Tamsin nodded.

"Just sayin'."

Susannah frowned as she tried to catch up. "So you're saying there are three possibilities here? One, that the contaminator is a murderer too,"

"Two, that someone was piggybacking on the contamination to follow their own agenda," added Tamsin.

"Three, that the murderer knew nothing about the yogurt or anything else," finished Emerald.

The three of them sat silently for a while with their thoughts, till Tamsin said, "Hey Susannah, were you serious about having to finish this cake?"

And Susannah gladly gave her another big helping of cake, Emerald protestingly accepted a small sliver, and the goatkeeper herself tucked into her creation happily. They turned the conversation to goats and the merits of wild-flower meadows and the quality of the hay you take from them till it was time to feed the kids again. And after more fun and frolics with the little goatlets, Tamsin and Emerald took their leave down the bumpy track, so pleased to have lightened Susannah's load.

CHAPTER SEVENTEEN

After a quiet day dedicated to her first love - actually training dogs, with two home visits out in the countryside, one for sheep-chasing and the other a dog who was afraid to cross the shiny kitchen floor, then followed up by her class at Nether Trotley - Tamsin had managed to push the artisan's problems out of her mind. And she felt there was nothing more she could do with the murder for now.

So on Tuesday morning over her second coffee of the day she was excited to see Maggie's number flashing on her silent phone. She snatched it up with a breathless "Yes, Maggie?"

"Got something that might be of interest to you. I'm ok to tell you - it's nothing to do with the murder."

"Ooh, goodie, I need something to work on!" Tamsin settled down with a pen and paper.

"They asked me to test some of these scones that were contaminated. I don't have much on and the labs are backed up. Fortunately the baker, Hilda, put them in the freezer when she got them back, just in case."

"Wise girl is our Hilda!"

"It was easy enough to locate the problem. It's a bitter substance they use to make products unpalatable to children and animals - things like antifreeze and detergent."

"Ohh, and pills?"

"Yes, definitely pills too."

"What is this stuff? Where do you get it? Is it dangerous?"

"Steady on! It's called denatonium. It's actually the most bitter chemical compound known. It's easy enough to get if you're in the business. And no, it's non-toxic. Anything else?"

"Yes! Where can I get a sample? I have an idea ..."

"Seeing as it's harmless I'll text you the info where to get it. Hope your idea is legal and not dangerous?"

"Oh, absolutely. Hey, could you just grind up some pills to get the bitter taste?"

"You *could*. But there would be a risk. If the wrong person took any of the medication that wasn't meant for them, it could have disastrous consequences."

"And our party-pooper doesn't seem to want to injure anyone. Just wreck the businesses of the makers. Actually, I'll tell you what I'll do! Before I follow up the links you're going to send me I'll just see what I can find out - as a non-scientific person, you know?"

"You're trying to see if *anyone* could have got hold of this stuff?"

"Ye-e-es. There's a person already in the frame, and he has a science background. Just seeing if we could widen the field. I'm thinking - as well as hunting online, I know a pharmacist in Worcester who'll be able to give me some info."

"Is there anyone you don't know, Tamsin?"

"Ha! It's another student. She had a boxer who was ripping the house to pieces. Been grateful ever since we sorted it."

"Dog now behaving himself?"

"Dog is a pet! We just had to find his anxieties and establish some boundaries."

"Boundaries. You spend your time keeping within them, while I spend mine dealing with people who've over-stepped them!"

"I'm not beyond crossing the odd boundary, if it's called for," grinned

Tamsin. "But dogs are happy knowing where they are and what's expected of them."

"Jez is very happy in his boundary - his bed! So you're going to find out how to .. find out, first of all? And then - tell me, what's your idea?"

"It's Banjo. I'm doing a lot of scentwork with him - he loves it! You know, the Search & Rescue stuff as well. And I'm just wondering if he'll be able to identify this substance. It's in antifreeze and detergent, you say?"

"They do tend to use denatonium for that. But I couldn't say whether it's in all those products."

"Ok. Useful for testing anyway."

"Are you thinking he could sniff it out at the market?"

"Well, Banjo's not mad about crowds so I don't know about that. Not sure what I'll do - just another thought!"

"I think you're trying to do me out of a job - and have my lab taken over by dogs in white coats ..."

Tamsin laughed loudly at the image. "Seriously, do you know how incredibly sensitive their noses are? They can sniff out a body in the bottom of a deep lake, from a boat on the surface! And they can detect cancer in five-year-old breath samples."

"That is astonishing. I've heard of them finding earthquake victims buried under tons of rubble. Perhaps I can have a 'Bring your dog to work' day and have a fleet of them sniffing."

"Sounds good to me! You'll need an expert trainer," laughed Tamsin, always ready to expand her business.

"Your dogs are so clever, Tamsin! Dear old Jez can sniff out his food bowl alright, and he actually chewed the bottom out of one of Don's pockets the other day, when his jacket was hanging over the back of a chair."

"Treats in the pocket?"

"There were."

"There you go, Jez's nose is in perfect working order!" Tamsin grinned as she rang off and waited for Maggie's text to arrive.

She jumped to her laptop meanwhile and, imagining herself to be the contaminator, she started hunting - not for 'denatonium' but for 'bitter tastes'. She wandered down a few cul-de-sacs and kept changing her search terms till she started to get the answers she needed. After fifteen minutes of frustration she grabbed her phone and tried phoning her pharmacist friend. With no reply she texted her and with a big stretch she jumped up from the table and said, "Let's go out guys!"

She didn't have to ask twice!

The flurry of activity and whirring tails was captivating - except for Opal who was dislodged from her snoozing spot in the middle of the very largest dog bed by a scampering Moonbeam, causing her to strut away, tail in air.

Unsurprisingly, after a walk in the baking hot sunshine, Tamsin and her dogs found themselves entering the cool of The Cake Stop. But she pulled up short outside the door where there was a dog water bowl on the pavement with a blackboard beside it bearing the words:

SCORCHIO!
Water for the DOG
Or short people
with low standards.
We don't judge

Laughing happily, she ordered her coffee at the counter. "Love your sign, Kylie! That's your handiwork I'm guessing?"

Kylie smiled, her cheeks dimpling. "The water's probably warm by now. I'll change it in a minute. But yours can have some cold water here, and she pointed out the water bowl she'd put down for visiting dogs just by the counter.

"How kind!" said Tamsin, as the dogs took turns to glug their way through the water. "You're very thoughtful." And she settled her dogs in their favourite window corner, having completely caved in and ordered cake - after all it was two whole days since she'd scoffed Susannah's strawberry sponge cake.

"I'll bring it over - you've got your hands full," Kylie had offered. And it wasn't long before her coffee and a huge helping of pistachio meringue arrived at the table.

"Wow, the Furies have excelled themselves this time," she said, grasping the spoon. "I haven't seen this one for a while."

"They've got a few different ones coming. Getting very imaginative in their old age - in fact, this looks like Damaris arriving with our order right now," and Kylie raced to the big glass front door and held it open for the diminutive caterer.

Damaris chattered like a little bird as she lifted cake containers off her trolley and Kylie took them to a safe space back in the pantry area. And once she'd emptied her trolley she looked round the café, spotted Tamsin and hopped her way, bird-like, between the tables to join her.

"My *dear!*" she said as she looked questioningly at the empty chair at the table.

"Damaris! How lovely to see you - do sit! As you can see I'm just polishing off your delicious pistachio meringue. It is simply gorgeous!"

Damaris perched on the edge of the chair and simpered. "I'm so glad you like it. That one was actually my idea! I must tell Penelope and Electra. I see they've almost run out already," and she nodded towards the counter where Kylie was already placing some of the new cakes in place, including the new Mocha cake that Tamsin had sampled the previous week at the Furies' home.

"Not surprising. It's scrumptious."

"Oh, hello doggies! You have them all with you today?" Damaris's attention caused a brief flurry of wagging tails and smiling faces.

"Yes, we've had a great walk and a swim in the pond to cool down - at least they have! Not me. And how are you all doing? Have you heard any more about this food scare?"

"We have," chirped Damaris, sitting even further forward in her chair, her thin little legs swinging like a child's. "There have been more cases."

"Oh Lord. I've heard of a few. This nutcase needs stopping, but it's hard to find him .."

".. or her."

"Of course. Him or her. Who have you heard of?" And they compared notes as to who had been targeted. Apart from one apple juice person who'd only just discovered they'd been affected since the last market, there wasn't anyone new to Tamsin.

"You know what, Damaris? These people all attend the Farmer's Market, at least occasionally. It really seems to be a grudge against these folk."

"But who would know what to put in the foods, so they wouldn't actually hurt anyone? Because it seems that no-one has fallen ill."

"The worst case was the itching powder in the shawl - but that would have been temporary. Well," and now Tamsin leant forward in her chair, "I've been doing a bit of research."

Damaris clapped her hands and bounced in her seat, "Ooh, I knew you would! What have you been researching, dear?"

"They've found out what the substance put into Hilda's scones is, and I've been finding out how easy it would be to get hold of it, if you didn't have scientific knowledge."

"And?"

"And it's not that easy to discover or locate. You'd probably have to know what you were looking for. When you order it you have to accept certain warnings. You could buy it in a form that's already being sold - like a bitter spray to stop nail-biting - but you'd have to know."

"So you think that it has to have been done by someone with some level of pharmaceutical knowledge?"

"It looks that way. And there's one prime suspect." And Tamsin told Damaris about the scene in the market between Felicity and the disgruntled John Curtin with his science background.

Damaris frowned. "How awful. To do that to those people - it's not their fault that he was rejected!" The diminutive baker looked scandalised.

"I don't think rationality comes into it. Thing is, it all points to him, but unless the police can raid his house and find the stuff -"

"- or catch him red-handed!"

"Indeed. We're a bit stuck."

"How about," Damaris frowned even harder, "How about if you set something up at the market?"

"To trap him?"

"Yes! You remember Penelope's story about the wartime baker and the nuts and bolts? Well, she was remembering more of the story over supper that night. They took turns to keep a watch on her working, and caught her slipping a rusty old hinge into a loaf. Perhaps you could do something similar?" suggested Damaris eagerly.

"Hmm. We'd have to follow him round the market - always assuming he comes next Saturday. But Hilda's scones were injected in the shop - and Susannah's yogurt was contaminated at her Open Day."

Damaris looked dejected. "Oh dear, you're right. Are the police doing anything?"

"There have been no new instances since last week so perhaps they're watching and waiting. Though they have examined the scones - they *are* taking it seriously. Especially since the murder!"

"Are they connecting the two events?"

"They started off by scaring Susannah half out of her wits, but seem to have dropped that line of enquiry. I'm trying to keep my nose clean with Chief Inspector Hawkins by keeping out of it!"

"We've known Mabel Carstairs for *years*. Penelope is quite convinced it's the nephew." Damaris sat back and folded her arms across her flat chest.

"So that would suggest the murder had nothing to do with the contaminations, as he lives in Cambridge or London or somewhere. You see .. we wondered first of all if it was connected - you know, the contaminator actually wanted to kill Mabel - then we thought maybe someone was piggybacking on the scones and yogurt to get rid of her. And it seems, if it was the nephew, that it had no connection at all." Tamsin's mouth fell open as she stared into space. "UNLESS!"

"Unless what, dear?"

"Unless it's all there to confuse! And the whole thing's been set up to kill *another* person."

Damaris chewed her lip for a moment. "That's a bit convoluted isn't it, Tamsin? I mean to say, the more someone does, the more there's a trail for the police to follow. More likely to get caught."

"You're right, Damaris. It would be pretty stupid. But then, people who do these things don't tend to think sensibly. And I fear it's catching! Perhaps I should stick to what I'm good at, and train some dogs."

And so saying, she gathered up her gang, gave Damaris a hug and set off to leave the cool café ready for the wall of heat that would hit her as she went out of the door.

CHAPTER EIGHTEEN

When Emerald floated down the stairs with Opal padding down beside her the next morning after her hour of yoga, she found Tamsin with an array of cloth squares on the floor, and one held in her hand, gently, just by its corner. Banjo, ears up and eyes bright, was waiting for his moment.

"Wotcher doing?" said Emerald.

"Just doing some scentwork with Banjo. Can you hold off the coffee for a minute? This is our last run."

So Emerald sat on the stairs to watch, Opal on her lap slightly dismayed at the delay in reaching her food bowl.

Tamsin held out the cloth dangling from her hand to Banjo, who sniffed it carefully, his eyes crossing as he peered down his nose at it. When he'd got plenty of the scent, his tail started to swish excitedly. Then she quietly said, "Find!" and the dog started working his way round the cloths, sniffing audibly. He paused over the third cloth, went forward to the next, sniffed the last two, then came back and sat firmly pointing his nose at the third cloth.

"Fantastic! Good boy Benjo Banjo!" Tamsin danced about as she tossed the dog his favourite toy and started collecting up the cloths, putting them all straight into the washing machine.

"He did it right?" asked Emerald, by now used to the fact that these cloths had always to be clean, as she organised Opal's breakfast and filled the kettle.

"He did it ever so right!" beamed Tamsin. "What he did was locate the cloth with a tiny drop of antifreeze on!"

"Er, antifreeze?"

"You remember, it's one of the products they put denatonium in, to make it taste bitter. And on the cloth in my hand I had a tiny, tiny drop of denatonium."

"So he was able to detect the bitter stuff inside the antifreeze? That's amazing!"

"It sure is. Dogs' noses are awesome. Let's have coffee under the ash tree, and I'll tell you what I have in mind."

And as they settled in the shade of the leafy tree, the dogs mooching around till they found a cool spot to lie in - except for Banjo who was still excitedly tossing and catching and bouncing his ball on a string after his successes - Emerald said, "He learnt that incredibly quickly. Is it that he's a genius, or you are?"

"Neither!" laughed Tamsin. "It's just a question of steadily teaching it and practicing it. You know I've been doing a lot of scentwork with him since we started volunteering with Search & Rescue? Well, it's just a case of doing more of it, and with different scents. Technically, what he's doing here is called "scent discrimination" as opposed to plain searching. He's looking for the scent that matches the one I've asked him to find."

"What a dog! Here, I've been thinking,"

"Steady on!" laughed Tamsin, but smiled broadly at her friend.

"I have been thinking," Emerald repeated firmly. "And what I thought was - how about talking to Rose in *Health in the Hills*? I'm sure the police will have talked to her about Hilda's scones, but .. you never know .. could be worth an ask?"

"You *have* been thinking! And that's something I never thought of. Yes! Let's go up and talk to her. I've already walked the dogs before it got too hot, so we can drive up. We need to do a shop anyhow. The cupboards are bare and the fridge just has some squishy tomatoes and wilted lettuce."

"And something nameless at the back, wearing a fur coat. I chucked it out yesterday evening," Emerald made a face.

The health shop was not as well-equipped as The Cake Stop, and didn't have air conditioning, but there was the welcome whirr of a fan as they entered.

"Have you got Mrs.Bun the Baker's wife?" a loud voice came from the little café area.

"No dear, but I want you to give me Master Collier the Coalman's son!"

"Good Heavens," Tamsin said quietly to Emerald, "I wondered if we'd stumbled on a kidnapping!"

"It's *Happy Families!* We used to love playing that as kids. Look, it's that trio of old ladies over in the corner."

"Here every bloomin' morning," said Rose, leaning on the counter amidst the tea things, flicking her tea-towel about in a desultory fashion.

"Hello Rose! Glad to hear the café's going well. Different kind of appeal from the coffee shops in town."

"Tea and buns. That's what we do here. Linda wanted to make it different. There's folks who wouldn't be caught dead in a *la-di-da* coffee shop - my Mum for a start!" she snorted derisively. "We have a lot of regulars."

"Clever marketing!" said Tamsin as a howl of triumph from the ladies' table signified that someone had collected a whole family and won the game. "Actually, scones was what I wanted to talk to you about."

Streetwise Rose narrowed her eyes and stood up straight. "Oh yeah?" she asked cautiously. "Them police have been in here grilling me. I told them everything I knew."

"I'm sure you did, Rose. And I know you're pretty observant. But I just wanted to check a couple of things - is that ok?"

Rose frowned, shrugged, tossed the tea-towel onto the counter and folded her arms.

"Ok. This is what I was wondering. When you get a delivery of scones or buns or whatever, are they brought to you here at the counter?"

"S'right. And if you mean Hilda's scones, why don't you say so?"

"I do, you're right. Does she bring them in a box? Or on a tray?"

"In a box. And I puts them on display here." Rose waved to the acrylic cabinet on the countertop containing plates of buns, scones, and other wholesome baked fare.

"Oh, so the scones went inside there?" Emerald went over to look more closely at the display case.

"Nah. That's new. Linda bought it after the business with Hilda's scones."

"Oh, so it's new! Where did the scones go before you got that?" asked Tamsin, slightly relieved that this complication was removed, and marvelling how hard it was to get straight answers out of wily Rose.

"Just here. On the counter - that thing weren't there. People could help themselves. Now I has to do it." Rose sighed her most put-upon sigh.

"Right. That's a wise move of Linda's. So anyone could have leaned over the plate and .. interfered with the scones."

"Yeah. I s'pose."

"How long were they there before they were all sold?" Emerald asked.

"I dunno, do I! Not long. They goes fast, does those scones. Mebbe an hour or two. It was them ladies over there who complained."

"The card-players?"

"Yer. Hilda was ever so upset when she came in to collect them all."

"I'm sure she was! Tell me, Rose, would you have many people in here at that time?"

"I know what you're getting at, Mrs.Dog-Lady. You wants to know if I saw whodunit."

"That's right!" Tamsin smiled at Rose, loving her quaint new moniker. "Can you cast your mind back to that day and think of anyone - anyone at all - who was in here, who isn't usually."

"Perhaps someone you hadn't seen before?" prompted Emerald, as Rose furrowed her brow and thought hard.

They waited expectantly.

"Nah," said Rose, eventually, shaking her head with finality.

Tamsin's shoulders slumped. She tried a new tack. "I remember you saying you get few men in here."

"Oh, you want to know about the men too?"

"Er, yes?"

"Well there was that old German geezer. The one who comes in every day for his scone and 'appricot yam'. He comes in just after Hilda delivers."

"Does she always deliver at the same time?"

"More or less. But I found out," Rose spoke confidentially, "he lives over the piano shop over there." She jerked her head towards the music shop over the road.

"Ah, so he watches out for the fresh scones!"

"Yer. He does."

"You have an amazing memory, Rose!" Emerald felt the time was right for a bit of flattery.

The little shop assistant rose to the bait. "That's not all I remember! There was this other geezer. Smallish bloke. Bit bald on top, you know? He was faffing around with the leaflets over by the door, and creeping round the whole shop. Eventually he came over and bought a coffee."

Tamsin's ears pricked up, just like Moonbeam's. "Did he buy a scone?"

Rose frowned and twisted her mouth expressively. She turned and looked at the coffee machine, and eventually said, "Nah. He asked for almond milk, so I had to wash the jug and open a new carton from the fridge over there."

"So he distracted you?"

"I had to get the milk, didn't I?"

"Of course you did! So the German man had his scone as usual, then the other man came in?"

"Yep."

"Then the card ladies got theirs?"

"They'd already had their first round. They wanted more. They was sorry they did, as they tasted vile."

"Rose, you're a marvel. Did you tell the police about this man?"

"Nah, they never asked, did they. Just wanted to know where the scones were kept, like."

"Do you like any of these cakes, Rose?" Tamsin pointed to the cabinet.

"Them doughnuts are nice."

"Let me buy you one. Two - one for later," and she fished her purse out of her pocket. "You've been really helpful!"

"I knew you had Miss Herring the Fishmonger's daughter!" a loud voice broke in accusingly from the card table.

"I'm sorry dear, I didn't see it. I think it got a bit of jam on it and it stuck to the back of Mrs.Soot, the Chimney-sweep's wife."

Tamsin and Emerald laughed happily, and even sullen Rose cracked a smile as they went out through the shop door, the bell jangling as they reached the hot pavement.

CHAPTER NINETEEN

Tamsin finished feeding the dogs and started supper, fortunately with replenished supplies so the wilted lettuce could be left out for the birds.

"I think a pow-wow with Feargal is called for," she said as she picked up her phone and began texting him.

After a bit of tapping and lip-chewing, she tossed the phone aside and checked the saucepans. "Oh, you've done the salad already! Thanks Em."

"What did Feargal say?" Emerald tossed her blonde hair back over her shoulder and placed the bowl on the table.

"I'm meeting him at Jean-Philippe's tomorrow on my way to see Teal the troublesome Springer Spaniel."

"Ahh!" Emerald flashed her eyes meaningfully. "Jonathan's dog," and nodded.

"Yes, Jonathan's dog," said Tamsin firmly. "Anyway it'll be around two - you free?"

"Oh no, I have a couple of privates tomorrow afternoon before my Thursday evening class."

"Pity. It was the only time he and I could both make it. I'll let you know what he's learnt."

So with her training bag packed with irresistible treats for Teal safely stowed in the Top Dogs van, she breezed into the coffee shop.

"Hi Jean-Philippe!"

"*Mais bonjour, Mademoiselle* Tamsin," he replied, nodding to the darker depths of the café where Feargal sat with a small mountain of food and two mugs of coffee.

"Oh thanks, Feargal!" she said as she flopped into the chair and took a big glug of coffee, averted her eyes from his plates of food and sat back.

"You don't think I'm going to eat cake while you don't, do you?" he smiled a crooked smile and handed her a fork, pushing the plate bearing the new Mocha cake towards her.

Tamsin had the grace to blush before grabbing the fork from her friend's outstretched hand and tucking into the cake, then pushing the plate back towards him so they could share. And after some contentedly bovine - or perhaps, more fittingly, caprine - munching, she sat back and slapped her tummy with both hands.

"Ahh, that's better! I had a sneak preview of that cake last week. Superb. So. What news, young newshound?"

"I've been sniffing around Reggie Carstairs and what he does in Cambridge and how he's connected with the Science Park. And yes, it's interesting alright!"

Tamsin cocked her head attentively.

"He's involved in some hush-hush research into laser beams and specially-ground lenses. Combining the two to make a more powerful tool. Possibly a weapon."

"That's all new?"

"Not exactly. They use lenses with lasers already. This is something to do with focussing the laser to pinpoint accuracy, so it can penetrate mirroring materials. They're used in defence."

"Wow. I'm blissfully unaware of all this kind of thing. Very hush-hush, I imagine."

"That's why he comes over here sometimes. He's collaborating with another team on the same research. And do you remember one of the applications of thallium?"

"Lenses!" Tamsin gasped.

"Yep. He could certainly have access to the poison."

"Hmm. Well, I've been learning more about John Curtin. It seems that someone who answers his description was snooping about the health shop the morning Hilda's scones were attacked. He distracted Rose long enough to be able to wham a needle into a few of them."

"How did he do that?" Feargal nodded to the cake display cabinets on the countertop where Kylie was serving a customer.

"They used to just be there, naked, on the counter. Not any more. They're behind perspex now, like these ones."

"That's pretty damning evidence from Rose. Circumstantial, but accurate, I'll bet. What did the police make of it?"

"Astonishingly, she didn't tell them. She comes from the kind of background where you don't volunteer information to 'the rozzers'."

"That's our Rose!" laughed Feargal. "What's your next step?"

"I'm going to go up to the Farmers' Market on Saturday to see if he turns up there. I'll have Banjo with me - you won't believe how clever he is, so quickly, at detecting denatonium in substances!"

"I guess it's such a strong smell that he can pick it out easily."

"I've trained him on a tiny, tiny, drop. I don't want to put him off! But it seems humans are much more sensitive to it than animals, so I don't feel so bad."

"And you hope he'll pick out Curtin?"

"You know how Banjo hates crowds. So I'll stand away a bit with him, near the entrance to the market. And when it's quiet I may wander round and see if he can pick anything up on the stands."

"Our campaign at the *Malvern Mercury* seems to be taking effect. People are commenting to say they'll support these artisans through thick and thin. And of course there are people baying for the police's blood for not catching the person yet."

"So he may need to try harder to discredit them? At least they're all on their guard now, so it should be more difficult for him to get at their stuff."

"You're right though - he could well try it again. And what will you do if Banjo identifies him as having the substance about his person?"

"Citizen's arrest! I've always wanted to do that - now could be my moment!"

"Think he'll resist? Could he turn nasty? Remember he may be armed with a syringe."

"If I do that I'll be sure to be surrounded by loads of people. And if I do it in the right place, there will be so many infuriated stall-holders that he won't stand a chance of getting away."

"I've got to cover a footie match in Worcester on Saturday. My unfavourite thing. Short-staffed. Otherwise I'd be there ... Tell you what though! Remember Jeff, one of our photographers?"

"Course I do! He took some splendid photos of my Big Dog Walk."

"That's him. I'll tip him off - see if he can get down there and capture the occasion on film."

"That would be brilliant! And quite something for the *Mercury,* I can see. But I don't know when this may happen. Last time it was the afternoon when he showed up and started arguing. Don't know if he'll come at all this Saturday ..."

"Well, some pictures of happy crowds at the market will help with our campaign, so no worries."

"Ok. Sounds good. So I know what *I'm* doing next - what about you?"

"I'm going to do a bit of sniffing round Dolores's background. Not altogether happy about her. Who knows, she and Reggie may be in cahoots."

"Or maybe it was neither of them," Tamsin said glumly. "And if so, I have no idea who it could be. Did I tell you Emerald's idea?

"What was that? Oh, look who's here!" A scrabbling of dog paws on the wooden floor alerted them to the immediate arrival of Charity and Muffin.

"Muffin!" said Tamsin happily, always glad for an injection of canine enthusiasm. "Charity! You coming to join us?"

"I can't stop, dear. I saw you through the window and just thought I had to tell you. Muffy darling, get your paws off the table!"

Feargal pulled over a chair. "Tell us what, Charity?"

"My idea," she said breathlessly as she perched on the chair. "I've been thinking about all this awful business. Resentment, anger, all of that. And poor Mabel of course."

"Indeed, poor Mabel. What did she ever do to deserve this?"

"Exactly my dear. You've hit the nail on the head. You see, she didn't! Do anything, I mean."

Tamsin and Feargal exchanged glances, but knew they had to let Charity tell the story her own way.

"I don't think Mabel was the intended victim."

"It was an accident?"

"Not exactly, no. More of a dress rehearsal. For the real thing."

"Someone else is going to get murdered?" Tamsin gaped at Charity, and for a moment stopped stroking Muffin.

"That's what I think. That nephew of hers has plenty of his own money. I remember Mabel boasting about how successful he is - and I know his family left him plenty. I can't believe he'd bump off his aunt for a house in Malvern - albeit a large and expensive house."

"So what are you thinking, Charity?" Feargal asked quietly. He knew well that this slight old lady had such a wealth of experience behind her that she didn't come out with flights of fancy.

"Well, I think that not only is someone piggybacking on the damaged food to kill someone, but they're actually targeting someone else entirely, and Mabel was a dummy run."

"Muddying the waters with the yogurt, and even an unconnected victim?" asked Feargal.

"Yes. Smoke and mirrors."

"Very hard to make sense of," said Tamsin quietly. "Though as Damaris pointed out, the more they do the more chance there is of getting caught."

"That's very true. But it's a worrying thought, isn't it my dears, that with no idea who's doing this, we now have to wait for another murder!"

CHAPTER TWENTY

After Charity's suggestion, it was in a sombre mood that Tamsin opened the door of her van and waited a couple of minutes before touching the boiling hot driver's seat. She folded a towel to sit on and opened both windows to let the breeze blow the heat out as she drove, then shut them again and zapped on the air conditioning as she motored along the leafy back roads to Herefordshire and her home visit to the errant Springer Spaniel, Teal.

Jonathan was pleased to welcome her when she arrived at his home. "No dogs today?" he said, peering at her van.

"Way too hot! So you just have me," she smiled. "So this is your Cidery - could I have a look round?"

"Sure! This way," Jonathan led her towards some large barns. Her request wasn't just idle curiosity, as she was able to observe Teal as they walked round the place. After some lusty barking on her arrival, he was clearly just scared and kept away from this strange visitor. He was happy racing about the yard and buildings sniffing, and Tamsin was already formulating a training plan for the little dog.

The first place they visited was the fermenting area. A heavy scent hung on the air in the dark barn, the walls lined with ancient-looking wooden barrels and the centre of the floor full of fermenting vats and a few large timber crates of apples stored over the winter. Jonathan pointed out the barrels containing last year's cider, slowly maturing - before they left that barn and came to a building with a very modern appearance.

"He can't come into the bottling area, but he's safe enough out here in the yard," Jonathan explained as he ushered Tamsin into the brightly-lit bottling area.

He waved to the two people working amongst the shiny glass and steel shelving, such a contrast to the dark wood and strong scents of the fermenting area. "Here it's all about hygiene," Jonathan had to shout to be heard over the clank of glass bottles, "whereas in the fermenting sheds it's all about flavour - that's why we use oak barrels."

"So the oak makes the cider taste different?" asked Tamsin, fascinated.

"It does. Some producers prefer chestnut. But I think oak enhances our particular cider apples." He held the door open so they could emerge into the bright sunshine and comparative quiet outside.

"It's not just science, then?"

"Oh goodness me, no! Cider-making is an *art!*" said Jonathan proudly as he whistled to Teal, who emerged from the back of a shed with sawdust adorning his muzzle. "Been after the mice again?" he laughed.

"Don't the inspectors baulk at mice in the production area? I presume you're inspected?"

"Inspected to death, yes. Mice are everywhere in the countryside, we just make sure they don't get into the clean areas. Did you notice the mouse brushes on the bottom of the doors in the bottling plant?"

"I did actually! Susannah has those on her doors to the dairy. So that's what they're for! I did wonder."

"It's impossible to make these old doorways plumb, and the little fellas hate squeezing through a gap with rough bristles! I've nothing against mice, so long as they observe the social niceties," he smiled, and they made their way into the house to start Teal's lesson.

Jonathan watched with admiration while Tamsin encouraged shy Teal to engage with her - helped by some tasty morsels of chicken - to the stage when he was happy to play games with her. She showed Jonathan how to do some basic nosework with the little dog.

"It's what they're bred for - using their nose. And it's hugely satisfying for them."

"You're right: he always has his nose on the ground."

"So we can use this to help him to greet visitors - when you want them to be greeted. He doesn't need to meet casual delivery men and the like." And she demonstrated a way to encourage Teal to quickly sniff a visitor's hand to get all the information he needed about them to allay his fears.

By the end of the session, Teal was happily bouncing forward to sniff any hand held out for him, his fast spaniel tail with its lovely feathering swishing appreciatively.

"That's amazing! Thank you so much! Now we have something to work with, don't we, Teal Boy?" He ruffled the dog's ears and raised an inquiring eyebrow to Tamsin. "Coffee?"

"Love it! I've never been known to refuse a good cup of coffee," she smiled, and feeling her cheeks dimpling, she blushed slightly and started packing away her dog training things.

They learnt a lot about each other over coffee - about how Tamsin had come to be in Malvern, and how long Jonathan's family had worked this apple farm - and sure enough, the conversation turned to the latest crime wave.

"Any more trouble with your corks?"

"No, thank goodness. Last Saturday I made sure to keep all the crates right at the back of the stand where no-one could reach them. And I only brought a couple of crates at a time and just went and unloaded some more from the car when I needed them. Everyone was on edge, and keeping an eagle eye on their stock. But nothing more seemed to happen."

"Let's hope their vigilance prevents any more."

"Got any further with this old lady who died?"

"N-no, not really. I've spoken to a few people involved with her. There was an idea that it was to do with her will, which means the nephew would be in the frame. But I really don't think it was him."

"What do the police think?"

"That I don't know. I'm trying to keep out of their way, having got a firm wigging from the Chief Inspector before."

"I heard that they were grateful for your input?" He raised an inquiring eyebrow.

Tamsin wondered who he'd been talking to. "I think we have an uneasy truce," she smiled. "And now I must be on my way. There's someone I want to talk to again, and I think it may be important." She held up a hand to forestall questions. "I'll tell you more if I find anything out that the makers need to know. Perhaps at our next lesson?" And they arranged another date as she handed over some nosework guides, went over the homework again, and Jonathan settled up.

As she drove back to Malvern along the back lanes she always chose in preference to the busier roads, she inhaled the scent of the roadside flowers through her open windows. Cow Parsley, Morning Glory, bramble flowers, Meadowsweet, and all the fresh green leaves, mixed together to make a heady scent - but light and refreshing compared with the heavy scent of the fermenting room.

What Charity had said had stuck in her mind. Emerald with one of her shafts of perspicacity had thought along similar lines. While the artisans' problems seemed to be abating, she had an unpleasant feeling in the pit of her stomach that Charity could - as so often - be right, and someone else was in danger. She racked her brains to find the connections, and knew that she had to talk to Dolores again.

CHAPTER TWENTY-ONE

Tamsin had driven straight to Dolores's house after her session with Teal, but there was no sign of life there. Needing to press on to see her other clients, she resolved to try again the next morning. She didn't know how soon the agency would have given Dolores a new client, but didn't want to leave a note to pre-announce her visit. The element of surprise was valuable!

But on Friday she was in luck. And soon after 11, in answer to her knock on the door, a straight-faced Dolores invited her in without enthusiasm.

"Thank you so much for seeing me again," Tamsin said as they sat once more at the sticky oilcloth-covered table in the lacklustre, somewhat grimy, kitchen. The smell of cat was almost overpowering, and she wondered how someone with so little interest in normal levels of hygiene was entrusted with looking after vulnerable invalids and old people. Perhaps this agency of hers needed to brush up on its background checks!

"You see," she continued, as Dolores said nothing, "I was wondering who else may have visited Mabel in the last few weeks. The police aren't releasing any details about how she died," she crossed her fingers behind her back, "and speculation is rife that it was the yogurt that killed her! I really want to help these craft people. Their livelihoods are at risk while people think they're going around killing their customers!"

Dolores absently stroked the cat that had parked itself on her lap, and began to look less hunted and more interested. "Well there was the tea party she held for some of the artisans a couple of weeks back."

Tamsin was gobsmacked! How had Dolores not thought to mention this before?

"Something to do with the WI."

"The Women's Institute?"

"Yeah. She wanted to arrange some talks and invited a few of them round to discuss it. It was a kind of general invitation - for anyone interested, you know? She put the word out at the Craft and the Farmers' Markets. She had me make sandwiches."

"Who came?"

"Dunno. I don't know these people. Let me think .. There was a woman called Fiona or Freda or Felicity who seemed to be in charge of the markets. Then there were some dumpy women - don't know what they made. There was .. uh .. a butcher - he brought along some little cooked sausages for everyone. Oh, and someone who did metalwork. Baldish chap."

Tamsin's ears pricked. "Can you remember any names, apart from Felicity?"

Dolores screwed up her eyes in thought. "One of the dumpy women was called Hilda, never stopped eating. Can't remember the other - she was all bedecked with woolly shawls despite the fact it was early summer and already quite hot. The butcher I don't know. Oh, and Curtin, that was the bald geezer. Yes. I thought what an odd name, to be called after a curtain." She looked slyly up from her cat to Tamsin, who didn't miss her expression but passed no remarks.

Tamsin thought to herself, so Dolores wants to throw John Curtin under the bus! Why? What does she know? And aloud she said, "So how did the party go?"

"Oh, so-so. There was a bit of ganging up, I could see. Factions, you know? I heard two of the women pointing out the bald guy and complaining to each other that he was there. I was passing round the sandwiches you see. They didn't seem to like him, thought he was gate-crashing."

"Did he talk to any of them?"

"Now you come to mention it, no. He did approach the manager woman, but she didn't welcome him and introduced him to Mabel so she could move off. One time I found him in the kitchen. He said he was looking for the toilet."

Curtin well and truly shafted, thought Tamsin, and changed tack. She nodded to the picture of the Spanish seaside village, and asked, "Tell me, what made you leave that lovely place and move to rainy old England - although we could certainly do with a drop of rain right now!"

"Usual stupid story. I met a man. He was holidaying and I was waiting tables. It was a holiday romance that lasted for a few years. But once we were married and I started to put on a bit of weight he completely lost interest. He'd chase after anyone slim and pretty." Dolores gazed at the picture. "I was slim and pretty once … but it seemed I didn't look the same in a cold and wet country."

"And is that how he left? Chasing someone?"

"It was. She led him on something awful. Then dropped him like a stone. Ghastly woman, landed me in all sorts of trouble. That's when he left me, his job, England. Didn't pay the mortgage of course, so I lost our house. Now I've got this place." She cast her eyes upwards hopelessly. "Dunno where he is now, and I don't really care." She stood up, one of the cats leaping off her lap as she scraped the chair back. "Got to go now. Did you get what you wanted from me?" She tilted her head and looked sideways at Tamsin.

"I did, thank you," Tamsin smiled prettily. And 'Oh yes!' she thought, as she waved goodbye at the front door, inhaling the cat-pee-free air of the hot summer's day.

She drove back to Pippin Lane in thoughtful mood. The dogs were delighted with her return, and she assured them that their time for a walk would come much later tonight, when it was cooler. She'd been including the "No dogs in hot cars" lecture in all her classes recently, and she settled in the shade of the ash tree in the garden, sipping some of Emerald's home-made lemonade and making a mental note to water the herb garden later on that night.

"Well dogs," she began, as she opened her notebook and started writing. "As I see it, Dolores is trying to put Curtin in the frame. Why?" She drew a big question mark. "Because she doesn't like him? Why?" Another big question mark. "Because she genuinely thinks he did it? Why?" Another. "Because she just needs to shift the blame and it was really her? WHY?" She added three question marks, underlined the word WHY and sighed loudly.

Quiz walked over slowly and rested her chin on Tamsin's knee, her clear brown eyes gazing up at her. Her face seemed to be saying, "I wish I could help you, but I have no idea what you're talking about." And she accepted an ear-ruffle of her one upright ear before plodding back to the shady grass and flumping down with a sigh. She'd done her best.

"I think," Tamsin continued to the dozing dogs, "that I need to let that all swim about in my mind for a while and see what comes up to the surface - oh!" she said, as Opal floated up onto her lap, rubbed her face vigorously against her hand and purred loudly. "You've come to help me think it out, have you, Opal? Or - more likely - you want me to act as your own personal tin-opener! It's too hot for cats on laps," and she gently poured Opal back onto the ground.

As Tamsin leaned back in the chair she gazed at the silhouette of the Worcestershire Beacon which she could see up above her home, and picked out a couple of tiny figures walking along the ridge. "Bet it's hot up there," she said drowsily, as she followed her dogs' example and nodded off into a soothing nap.

CHAPTER TWENTY-TWO

Saturday morning dawned a little fresher than usual, though still very hot. They were all getting used to the unusual sight of a deep blue cloudless sky, for days on end. People had sunburnt noses and shoulders through spending too much time in the unaccustomed brilliant sunshine. English people tend to race into the sun without too much delay - in case they miss it!

So Tamsin was keen to set off to the Farmers' Market before the heat of the day set in, as she'd have Banjo with her.

"Come on slowcoach!" she called up the stairs to Emerald. "Are we going or what?"

Emerald somehow always managed to look super-cool and today was no exception. She wafted down the stairs wearing a green dress that floated around her legs in their sensible strappy sandals, a long silver cord draped around her hips to gather the folds of fabric in. The general impression was of an Arthurian princess from Camelot. Tamsin glanced down at her turquoise Top Dogs shirt and blue shorts and sighed. She knew she could never look like Emerald, not in a million years.

"You look smashing!" she said appreciatively as the cat trotted down the stairs beside Emerald. "Pity you can't bring Opal, her cream fur looks stunning against that frock."

"She'd probably quite enjoy it - she loves being the centre of attention, that right, Opal?" smiled Emerald. "Banjo ready for his work?"

"We've been practicing all week - as ready as can be, aren't you, Banjo Bunny!"

"Ok, let's go."

The Malvern Hills were sparkling in the sunlight and towered above them as they walked into town. The grassy areas on the Hills were pale brown and dry as tinder. "I bet the firewatch is busy in this weather."

"At least it's very easy to see as soon as a fire starts," Emerald reflected.

"Is true. You know they used to use the Hills as a firewatch base for all the surrounding counties during the war? You can see so far from up there, it was a great way to pick out flames at night and columns of smoke in the day."

"Thank goodness those days are over," said the peaceful Emerald with feeling, as they crossed the stream and started climbing up the hillside of the Common.

When they arrived in Great Malvern, they found that the hot weather had brought people out in their droves to visit the market. There was a bustle of people, children, dogs - all to the backdrop of the musicians enlivening the event with their foot-tapping tunes. This week there was an Irish céilí band, with fiddles and whistles and .. "What's that booming sound?" asked Emerald.

"It's a bodhrán. Sort of handheld Irish drum - lovely rhythms they make," smiled Tamsin, moving with the beat, relaxing into the festival atmosphere.

"Bow-ron," repeated Emerald, diligently learning the new word. "Boom-di-di-boom-di-di-boom! I love it!"

Emerald wandered in to look around while Tamsin and Banjo hung back up the hill away from the throng - which was something Banjo always found hard to manage, even more so if some small child cried

"Goggy!" and advanced, arms aloft, to try and pet him! That was one of the hazards of his blue merle coat and his blue eyes being so pretty.

So Tamsin occupied herself by looking down at the stalls and their busy customers, noting that some had no-one at all looking at them. She wondered whether their offerings were too expensive, too dull, or just not what people wanted. With her knowledge of marketing limited to promoting her dog training school and knowing what people thought they needed and what they *actually* needed, she realised these artisans and craftsmen had the same issue of matching what they wanted to make with what people wanted to buy. The everlasting conundrum: you have to find an area where what you enjoy doing and what people are prepared to pay for intersect!

"Oh look, it's Tamsin!" shouted a very young voice, and she was descended upon by three small boys and one Jack Russell Terrier. "Buster!" she laughed as Banjo slid behind her legs and Buster jumped about in front of her. "Hi boys! You getting some goodies for the weekend?"

"We are!" said Cameron, the oldest of the three.

"We want Mum to make chips, so she's come to get spuds," said Alex, the next one down, who was jumping about as much as Buster on the end of the lead he was holding.

"And we *saw* you!" squawked little Joe delightedly, pushing in front of Cameron.

"So where's Mum? Has she got Amanda in the pushchair?" Tamsin craned her neck to look amongst the stalls.

"Dad's taken her - look! There she is, on his shoulders!" Cameron pointed triumphantly.

And it wasn't too long till Chas and Molly came over with baby Amanda to join their sons.

"I can see why you had to carry Amanda," laughed Tamsin, nodding towards the pushchair that was crammed with all kinds of vegetables, bread, and goodness knows what else.

"I had to be careful with her on my shoulders not to bang her head on the rooves of the stands - it's easy to forget you're eighteen inches taller than usual! And how are you doing, Tamsin? Are you still doing the Nether Trotley classes? We'd like to book Buster in again."

"I am, and I'd love to see you there. Not giving you any trouble, is he?"

"No!" chorused the three boys together.

"No trouble," smiled Chas, "we just want to learn some new tricks. The boys are getting so good at teaching him."

"Perfect! Yes, drop me an email and I'll give you the next start date. We could teach him to fetch your car keys - would you like to teach him that, lads?"

"Yeah!" came the enthusiastic reply, as Cameron shoved Joe, and Alex nearly tripped over him.

"Hey boys," said Molly, "See how many times you can run round that great tree-trunk over there!" The boys hooted with glee and ran off to the tree - one of many ancient massive trees in the churchyard - with Buster, who was always up for anything. "I wanted to ask you, Tamsin," she said quietly once the children were out of earshot, "if you knew anything about this contamination scare."

"Er, I do actually .."

"Knew you'd be up to your neck in it!" Chas grinned.

"Well, I'm friends with one of the producers, that's why. It's awful for them. They work so hard to scrape a living from their stuff."

"And it's so good!" interjected Chas.

"It is," Tamsin agreed. "We think we might be on to something. Hopefully we can stop it, even if we can't pin anything on the person doing it. I'll let you know what we find out!"

"I ran round twelve times!" said a pink-faced Joe, tugging at his father's trouser-leg.

"No you didn't, silly," said Cameron, gasping for breath. "I ran round nine times and Alex ran round seven times, so you can't possibly have."

"I did so!" Little Joe stamped his foot.

"Boys, boys, boys!" Molly intervened before they started fighting. "I bought a beautiful cherry cake - who wants to get back home and tuck in?"

Three arms shot in the air, with shouts of "MEEE!"

"Meee!" echoed Amanda, still perched on her father's shoulders, holding onto his head.

"Lovely to see you all again!" and Tamsin watched as the busy young family tripped down the slope and made their way towards their car. She was still smiling as Emerald appeared, chatting to Jeff the *Mercury* photographer.

"Look who I found!" she smiled. "That Curtin fellow is down there," she flicked her head without turning, to indicate the middle of the market. "He's ranting at Felicity again. Really, I'd lose patience if it were me, but she seems to manage to hold it together. He's making it less and less likely he'll get a stall every time he has a go at her!"

"No prospect, I would think. Who'd want a misery like that cluttering up the market? Which way is he heading? I can try and intercept him with Banjo."

"I'll be out of sight, but I'll capture it all for you! I'm picking up lots of stock photos anyway," said Jeff, grinning conspiratorially as he edged away, hefting his big camera bag up on his shoulder.

Emerald walked quickly back down to the stalls and shortly arrived back, pointing towards the church. "That way!"

They all three went to the far end of the market, Jeff heading off in a different direction as he fitted a long lens to his camera, and sure enough - there was John Curtin, shoulders hunched, hands deep in his pockets, who'd stopped and turned round to glower at the market stalls.

Tamsin pulled a plastic bag from her pocket and opening it without touching the contents, offered her dog a sniff of the cloth inside. "Banjo, seek!" she said quietly.

Banjo's eyes sparkled - there's nothing a Border Collie likes better than working! - and started air-scenting. Tamsin moved behind their quarry, and Banjo's tail started to flip excitedly as he sniffed at his trouser-legs, then up towards his pockets. Satisfied, he went round in front of Curtin and sat, staring at him.

"Shoo! Go away!" said the man, flapping his hands at Banjo, who remained steadfast. This was his job and he was going to see it through.

Curtin saw the lead and as his eyes followed it up to Tamsin's hand said, "Get that dog away from me!"

"I think there's something you should know," said Tamsin imperturbably. "This is a trained sniffer dog. And the substance he's been trained to sniff out is denatonium."

Curtin blanched and began to stutter, "I - I don't know what you're talking about! Out of my way!" and he tried to push between dog and handler, only getting himself caught by the lead.

"I could make a citizen's arrest," Tamsin went on quietly. "But it's probably easier if I just tell the police who has been interfering with people's products and livelihoods." Her face was grim.

"You can't prove anything!" hissed the man, now feeling totally cornered.

Tamsin nodded towards Emerald, who was standing the other side of them filming the whole episode on her phone, and she spotted Jeff with his camera standing further away next to a stall. "It's all recorded. The dog identified you. I suggest you stop your nonsense before someone gets hurt."

John Curtin blustered and snorted, and this time managed to push past them, Emerald snatching the phone out of the way of his hand just in time. He stomped off towards the churchyard, and the two women turned and grinned at each other.

"Well!"

"This is fun!"

"Isn't it just? Banjo, you're a genius! Here, catch!" and she tossed him his favourite cloth frisbee and started tugging with him. "Hey, Molly bought a cherry cake - my mouth is watering. Shall we see what we can find before we go?"

And using the frisbee as a big distraction for Banjo, they managed to visit several stalls and fill their bags with goodies, receiving a silent salute from Jeff as he packed up his gear, before they started to trek home to Pippin Lane.

"A good job, well done, says I!" smiled Tamsin as they sat on the little bridge over the stream where Banjo splashed and played in the water.

"Operation Banjo a total success. Brilliant dog," and Emerald slowly shook her head in wonderment.

CHAPTER TWENTY-THREE

You can't give up all your Sundays to help me!" protested Susannah as the *Top Dogs* van wove its way up the pitted drive and trundled into the yard, the dust clouding behind it as it came to a slow halt.

"We're showing solidarity!" said Emerald as she jumped out of the van.

"And it's an educational visit for Banjo here," added Tamsin as she clipped the lead to Banjo's harness and hopped him out of the van. "He's the one who really loves other animals as long as there aren't too many people around."

"Ooh, I've been looking forward to meeting him! We'll have to introduce him to the older kids - they may like to have a romp."

"I've found a shady spot for the van - can I leave him here with all the windows and the back doors open till then? The crate doors I'll keep shut."

"Sure!" said Susannah, as Tamsin crossed the yard to give her a hug.

"Any news? We have some!"

"Well, no news is good news, I guess." Susannah shrugged. "There's been nothing more and I haven't heard a dicky bird from the police. Such a relief! What's your news?"

"We've identified the contaminator!"

"Oh, fantastic!" Susannah clapped her hands together and bounced up and down like a child. "That's wonderful news! So it's all over?"

"Hmm, hopefully. We were pretty sure it was him - John Curtin, that is - and Banjo confirmed it for us yesterday at the market."

Susannah tilted her head as if there was a huge question mark above it.

"Banjo's learning to be a sniffer dog! And his first task was to identify denatonium on this man."

"Dena-what?"

"The stuff that's making the foods taste bitter. Harmless, but nasty-tasting. Hadn't I told you that, sorry!"

"Oh wow! And Banjo could smell it?"

"Yep." Tamsin folded her arms and beamed proudly.

"So is he being arrested?"

"For now he's been warned off. Banjo's not officially qualified, you see, so the police would probably not accept his identification."

"But hey!" said Emerald, "as long as he stops, right?"

"That's such a relief! You are marvels, really. Fancy doing all this for us ..."

"Happy to help. We're both small business-people too. And reputation is so important, we know." Emerald put a hand on Susannah's arm.

"And we have good reason to know, as we've both been caught up in things that could have ruined us," Tamsin added, with a rueful expression.

"Fortunately, Tamsin on the war-path is not something malefactors ever want to see!" laughed Emerald.

"I'm very happy to see Tamsin on the war-path, any day! So how did that old lady die, if it wasn't from eating my yogurt?"

"Er, your yogurt couldn't have killed anyone. Denatonium is harmless. She was poisoned with something else."

"Poisoned?! Deliberately?"

"Yes. With a poison that's hard to get in this country."

"Oh my." Susannah looked fed up again. "So did this, this Curtin man - did he do that too?"

"We think probably not, though it's possible. But you don't need to worry about that - you're in the clear! Now, let's get stuck into some mucking out then introduce Banjo to the kids."

So Susannah armed them with bottles and they went to see their favourite goats. Having strawed some pens and filled the hay-racks, they emerged into the baking sun again plucking strands of hay off their clothes.

"Let's take Banjo round to the older kids," said Susannah as Tamsin hopped him out of the van and followed her as she led the way through some carefully-fastened gates to yet another paddock round the back of the farm buildings. They were greeted with much bleating, as if no-one had been there for a week. "In this weather they can stay out at night - saves me a lot of time mucking out pens."

Banjo sat beside Tamsin at the gate and studied the youngstock with interest. "Want to go in?" she asked, and his tail waved happily. So they all went into the field and in no time the kids and Banjo were running around, Banjo pretending to chase, running in big herding circles round the kids, and hopping over the tree-trunks and barrels that filled the paddock. The kids played King of the Castle as their hooves skidded on the smooth surfaces.

"He really loves this!" laughed Susannah, "Look at his smily face and lolling tongue." After a while - filled with giggles and laughter - they all headed back to the house, having enjoyed the spectacle.

"Bring him in, he'll want some water," said Susannah, holding the kitchen door open for them. And after guzzling water and leaving drips all round the water-bowl, Banjo threw himself flat on the cold flagstoned floor, panting lightly.

"I'm glad you turned up," she went on. "I've just been sent a gift and this is a perfect opportunity to open it."

"Ooh, what've you got?" said Emerald, peering at the box on the table.

"It's a box of chocolates! Well, not a box like you'd get in a shop. It's someone who wants to start off selling chocolates and they sent them to me to try out. They look pretty homemade, I must say. She may want to make some with goats cream, she says. She included this note." She lifted the typewritten note off and opened the box, showing a number of loose chocolates inside.

Tamsin stiffened. "You know this person?"

"No, I hadn't come across her before, but she says she saw me at the market one week and thought I'd be able to advise. Help yourselves!" She picked out a chocolate and raised it towards her mouth.

"Don't eat it!" Tamsin yelled as Emerald made a grab for Susannah's arm. Startled, Susannah dropped the chocolate and it bounced off the table and landed near Banjo's nose. Tamsin leapt from her chair as her precious dog opened his eyes and sniffed. *"Leave!"* she said firmly, scooping up the chocolate. Unperturbed, the dog closed his eyes again and went back to his snoozing.

"Oh my god! Do you mean this could have that bitter stuff in?"

"Worse. It could have thallium in," Tamsin said grimly, as she returned the chocolate to the box and went to the kitchen sink to wash her hands, beckoning Susannah over with a head movement to do the same.

"Thallium? Whatever's that?"

"It's the deadly poison that killed Mabel Carstairs. And no, these chocolates may be completely innocent, although still dangerous for Banjo."

Susannah gaped.

Emerald explained, "Some dogs die from eating chocolate. It's one of the first things Tamsin dinned into me when I moved in with her."

"I had no idea. But why would whoever killed that poor woman want to kill *me*?"

"This is a very good question. Tell me, you didn't know Mabel Carstairs?"

Susannah shook her head.

"What about her nephew Reggie?"

More head-shaking.

"John Curtin?"

"You just told me about him. Oh, I heard of him before! Wasn't he the fellow who was rejected for the market? I heard he turns up ranting at Felicity at every turn. Is that why he's been doing this?"

"Yes, that's him. How about Dolores?"

"Dolores?" Susannah looked blank.

"Know anyone in the WI?"

"Not my thing, I'm afraid. Seriously, I don't know if I know anyone who's in the Institute."

"You'd better give those chocolates to me," said Tamsin. "I'll take them to someone who can analyse them."

Susannah pushed the box over to her with a spoon, not even wanting to touch it now.

"I'll take that note too. Have you the wrapping it all came in?"

"It's in the recycling. Good thing it's so hot or it would have gone up in smoke in the Aga!" Susannah rummaged in the bin and produced a screwed-up ball of brown paper. She put it on the table to smooth out.

"No! Don't handle it. Have you got a plastic bag?"

Susannah left the room. "And sticky tape?" Tamsin called after her.

The shocked goatkeeper came back with a large black bin bag and a roll of tape, then sat at the table, chin on hands, looking glum.

Tamsin swept the box, the note, and the wrappings into the sack, parcelled it up and sealed it with the tape. "There!" she said, and washed her hands again.

"Don't worry, Susannah," said Emerald kindly, "They may be fine."

"And they may not," growled Tamsin. "I'm sorry to put a damper on a lovely day! Let's hope these chocolates are innocent. But just to be on the safe side, don't eat *anything* if you don't know where it came from! Pack it up like I just did and stow it somewhere safe."

"And tell us!" said Emerald, as poor Susannah nodded, then put a brave smile on her face.

And amongst many hugs, they loaded the possibly deadly parcel into the van under Emerald's feet, and Banjo into his crate at the back, and set off down the bockety drive. The last thing Tamsin saw was Susannah standing alone watching after them, clutching her arms around her, her hands gripping her elbows.

They stayed quiet in their own thoughts on the way home, and didn't relax till they had got inside and had an ecstatic greeting from the two remaining dogs and an aloof one from Opal.

"What are you going to do with those things?" Emerald gestured to the black bundle Tamsin was carrying.

"I'm going to put it up here," she replied, climbing up onto the kitchen worktop and wedging it securely amongst the dusty biscuit tins on the very top of the hanging cabinets. "And I'm going to text Maggie right now."

"While I put the kettle on," smiled Emerald.

"That's a fair division of labour!" Tamsin started tapping out a message on her phone.

A short while later as they nursed their coffee mugs in the cool of the living room, a buzz told them that Maggie had replied. Tamsin snatched up the phone, shifted Moonbeam off her lap and read out the reply.

"She says to drop it in to the station early tomorrow. She's there all morning. Right. Let's see if Susannah is another intended victim."

"It's an awful thought. But just too much of a coincidence that she got that more-or-less anonymous gift right now."

Tamsin shuddered and reached for Moonbeam again for reassurance. "She has a lovely place up there in the Hills. Those kids are such fun!" she laughed and smiled at Banjo, dozing on the hard floor and twitching his paws. "Look! Banjo's still playing with them."

CHAPTER TWENTY-FOUR

Tamsin dropped Emerald in Malvern Link for her first private session of the week and motored on down the hill to the police station. She had climbed up and released the black sack from its safe place just before leaving. She wasn't taking any chances with her beloved dogs!

While she waited in reception for Maggie to emerge, a familiar voice interrupted her reverie.

"Hello hello hello! What have we here?"

She couldn't believe that Chief Inspector Hawkins should parody the village plod so shamelessly - perhaps he had a sense of humour after all!

"Hello Inspector Hawkins," she gave a dazzling smile, which was not exactly reciprocated.

"Brought in some lost property, have we?" he glanced at the black parcel on her lap.

"Just doing my civic duty," she beamed. "Are you well? Got anywhere with these contaminations and poisoning?"

"Why are you linking those together, Ms Kernick?" he was suddenly all seriousness.

"Oh, just that they seem to be the same sort of thing ..." she shrugged.

"I hope I don't have to tell you again to leave policing to the police?"

"Not at all. No. Really you don't." She shook her head vigorously, then grinned and said, "But I bet you're glad that I didn't listen last time?"

Chief Inspector Hawkins sighed noisily. "One day you'll come a cropper," he turned away and said a few words to the constable on reception before sweeping out through the double doors of the station.

"He's right, you know," Maggie said quietly, having hung back listening to this exchange.

"I hope he's not!" said Tamsin with feeling. "Thanks for doing this, Maggie," and she handed her the black parcel. "When do you think you'll have a chance to test it?"

"I'll get back to you - probably later today. I'm mostly doing paperwork this morning."

"Talk to you later, then!" Tamsin gave a cheery wave as Maggie went back through the swing doors and she left the station and headed back to Pippin Lane to prep a couple of 1-1s and her Nether Trotley class tonight.

And while she chopped cheese and sausage into tiny bitesize pieces and sorted through handouts, she thought. Picking up her phone she texted Feargal.

Is there any link between Curtin and Susannah? Call me. I have news.

And fortunately he picked a time between her two home visits to get back to her. She'd just finished with an Irish Wolfhound who loved lying the full length of the sofa and growling when anyone else wanted to sit down, and was thinking ahead to the Patterdale Terrier later on that afternoon who was obsessed with snapping flies, when she saw his reply.

Cake Stop in 20?

"Yay, guys!" she said cheerily to her slumbering dogs, all stretched out on the hard floor, intent on keeping cool. "I'm off out again, for *cake!* See you later." And she grabbed her keys and left the house.

Feargal was amazed to hear the latest about John Curtin. "So can Banjo sniff out thallium as well?"

"*No!*" Tamsin slammed her forkful of cake down on her plate. "On the one hand, it's odourless. On the other hand, where would I get a deadly poison? And on the third hand, do you really think I'd let my precious dog anywhere near it?"

"Ok, ok," Feargal held his hands up in front of him to stave off her anger. "I didn't think of that, sorry. Of course not. But it's genius getting him to nail Curtin for the contaminations!"

"He went off with his tail between his legs, I can tell you! And if there's any more nonsense I *will* tell Hawkins." Feeling soothed, she resumed munching her carrot cake. "Anyway, there's more!" And she retailed the story of Susannah's chocolates.

Feargal shut his mouth and said simply, "Wow." He took a swig of coffee, and added, "So that's why you wanted to know if there's a connection between Susannah and this Curtin creep. And I found nothing. Nothing at all. That's not to say there *isn't* anything - just that I haven't found it."

"Right. I could be wrong, of course. I could have confiscated some perfectly harmless goodies from a hardworking goatkeeper - and frightened the life out of her!"

"You may have kept the life *in* her! No, you were good. Instinct is there to be followed. Any news from Maggie?"

"Not yet." Tamsin licked the last remnant of icing from her fork and sighed as she put it down on the empty plate. "Another cake, another few inches," she sighed.

The slim and lithe Feargal said, "With all the walking you do, you're fine. Enjoy your simple pleasures!"

"I would love everyone to continue enjoying their simple pleasures. And with another madman about, it's hard. If those chocolates were poisoned, then there's got to be some sort of link with Mabel. The only connections we have there are nephew Reggie and carer Dolores. I can't see that it could be either of them - or anyone else. Except ..." and she told Feargal about Mabel's tea-party.

"That would be the perfect time to poison something of hers. Who else was there?"

"Dolores wasn't clear. Curtin for definite. Also Hilda. And Felicity, you know, the market co-ordinator. Oh, and 'a butcher'. Probably that fellow I saw selling sausages and pies the other week. Other than them, she couldn't remember - or felt she'd fingered enough people to be going on with."

"Have they found out how the poison was administered yet?"

"Not heard anything. Hey, maybe this will tell us something!" and she scooped up her phone that was flashing and buzzing an incoming call.

"How did you know?" demanded Maggie's voice, as Tamsin answered. "What made you suspect?"

"Just a gut feeling, I'm afraid, Maggie. Nothing more. Do you mean to say ..?"

"Yes. Thallium. Enough to seriously disable in several of the chocolates. It was easy to see which, as there's a tiny hole on the underside of some of them."

"Good God." Tamsin looked helplessly at Feargal, who leaned over with head tilted, listening in.

"You realise I've had to hand all this over, don't you."

"Of course. Yes. Absolutely. Poor Susannah! Thank goodness I was there, nosey parker that I am."

"Very true. But seriously, I have to warn you Tamsin. Let the boys in blue take over now."

"I will. I've told Susannah not to consume anything she hasn't made herself."

"Same goes for you. If it's discovered you thwarted their plans, the poisoner may switch his - or her - attentions to you."

"Oh Lord. I hadn't thought of that."

"And I'd steer clear of Hawkins if I were you - he is *not* happy!" Maggie laughed as she ended the call.

Tamsin tossed her phone onto the table amid the coffee mugs and empty plates, and sighed noisily. "What do you think?"

Feargal winked. "I think I need to do some more sniffing about. Like Banjo, I'm a sniffer-hound!"

"Think you'll find anything?"

"Now it's a matter of life and death I'll make sure I find something."

"And I just have to deal with a terrier snapping flies. Mind you, that could be a life and death matter. His owner is afraid he'll snap a wasp or a bee!" She smiled as she stood up, slipping her phone into the pocket of her shorts. "Let me know what you find."

CHAPTER TWENTY-FIVE

Emerald and Tamsin were sitting under the ash tree, the ice clanking in their lemonade glasses. "This stuff is so refreshing!" said Tamsin as she drew patterns in the condensation on the side of her glass. The dogs were sprawled in the shade. Opal lay in the direct sun till it got too hot even for her and she slowly crawled under a bush and flattened herself.

"Thank Heavens we were there," Emerald said for at least the third time today. "I shudder to think what would have happened."

"All those poor goats ..." Tamsin immediately thought of the animals. "I believe if those heavy milkers aren't milked twice a day it can end in disaster."

"Not to mention all those hungry kids."

"Let's push these morbid thoughts out of our minds! All's well that ends well."

"But it hasn't ended yet!" wailed Emerald. "And we can't do a thing!"

"Don't you believe it," Tamsin said with a grim smile. "Feargal is on the case, and he's bound to find something. I only spoke briefly on the phone to Susannah yesterday, and she's baffled. She'd already had a visit from the police. They need to work fast."

"I've been thinking," said Emerald as she topped up their glasses noisily from the jug, some of the ice not yet melted.

"Uh-oh," teased Tamsin, then said quickly and seriously, "Is this another shaft of perspicacity from our serene Yogi?"

"Well." Emerald took a sip of her cool drink. "Poison is a nasty thing. I think it comes from a nasty mind. Where something has festered for so long that it's become poisonous too."

"I'd go along with that."

"So I wondered .. which of our possible suspects has an old secret that has been churning about inside them, maybe for years? Some ancient history perhaps, that they're blaming someone else for - whatever circumstance they're in now."

"Hmm. Hard to know. Especially as we haven't really got any suspects."

"I really like Susannah. And I love what she does. But, just supposing .. I mean, if we didn't know her or like her .."

"You're saying she could be doing it herself? She could have made those chocolates and waited for a suitable moment?"

Emerald nodded, a desperate expression on her face. "It *is* possible, though, isn't it?"

"She'd have known which ones were poisoned, and could have feigned illness in order to get them checked ... But why would she do that?"

"To appear to be a victim, not the poisoner?"

"And why would she want to poison Mabel Carstairs?"

Emerald tipped her sun-hat down over her nose, leant back in her seat and said hopelessly, "I don't know. I just thought we should look at it dispassionately. Other possibilities, you know?"

"You're absolutely right. We've been looking at it all too narrowly. We need to take our own feelings out of it. But .. Susannah?" Tamsin's astonishment showed in her face.

"Who else is there? We're seriously short of possibilities."

"I hope Feargal can come up with something. Otherwise we'll just have to sit and wait for Hawkins to crack the case."

"Something he hasn't managed to do without your help recently!"

"Is true. But they do have all the tech, and the forensics, and Maggie, and manpower, and the force of the law."

"And we just have our 'little grey cells'," laughed Emerald. "I'm glad you think my idea is silly."

"Not silly. Possible. But let's hope, unlikely. You want to keep washing in that soap, and the dogs and I love her yogurt." Tamsin stretched lazily. "I do believe it's even hotter today. I wonder when this extraordinary weather will break. It's certainly upping my tension levels!"

"Not only yours. I saw someone snap at poor Rosie in *Health in the Hills* yesterday," Emerald lowered Opal gently to the grass as she realised she'd been lying on her lap and was slowly cooking her.

"Was she upset?"

"Water off a duck's back for Rosie! But I was upset. I hate nastiness."

"Would all the world were like you." Tamsin smiled indulgently at her friend. "Hey, haven't you got class tonight?"

Emerald tipped her sun-hat back on top of her head. "Yup. At Jean-Philippe's. I always enjoy that class. Now."

"I'm glad you're looking forward again. You have a loyal bunch of students there too - even if some are a bit off the wall."

"Speak for yourself! Just how batty are some of your dog students?"

"*Touché!* You don't have a corner on nutcases. But they are fun, aren't they! We're always meeting new people. I think I might amble up with you for a coffee before your class. Catch up with a few of them."

"That would be nice."

"And when I get back it'll be cooling down enough to walk the dogs, I reckon."

"What's that noise? I can hear something." Emerald tilted her head.

"Oh, it's my phone. I left it in the kitchen. Better see what it is," and Tamsin got up lazily and went into the kitchen. Moonbeam jumped up to follow her and so did Banjo. Quiz simply opened one eye, took in the situation, closed it again and lay flat with a big sigh.

Tamsin emerged into the garden, studying her phone with a slight frown on her face. "It's a message from Feargal. He's found something out."

"Oh? What?"

"Um .. He wants to meet." She tapped quickly with her fingers and one thumb. Then sat down again with the phone in her lap. Another buzz, and she scooped it up to read the new message. "Yep, I suggested The Cake Stop at 5.30. He'll be there."

"Ok. Wonder what he has for us. I'll start getting ready in a while," and Emerald stretched her long limbs then relaxed again. "I could get used to this!" she laughed.

"Ye-e-e-s," said Tamsin dreamily. "But actually the glow is beginning to wear off for me. I don't do heat well. It's alright for you in your floaty dresses, but I need trousers with lots of pockets."

"There are dresses with pockets."

"Not big enough pockets for me. And skirts flap in the dogs' faces and get in the way. I think it should be a law that no garment may be sold unless it has serviceable pockets." She folded her arms and smirked. "Anyway, it's getting hotter. It has to break soon. It'll be a welcome relief."

But Tamsin wasn't to know how soon the weather would change, or what it would bring with it.

CHAPTER TWENTY-SIX

Tamsin decided to forego cake. Instead she ordered a syrupy, frothy, iced concoction that Jean-Philippe called a *café glacé*. "I don't know if this will pile on more inches than that lemon cake," she said to Kylie as she took her payment.

"Don't worry about that! You need your calories with all the walking you do," said Kylie kindly, with an eye to the café's takings as well.

Tamsin grinned, picked up the tray bearing Emerald's and her orders, and threaded her way through the dark mahogany tables to the back of the café. "It's quiet here," she put the tray down on the table.

"Quiet-*ish*," corrected Emerald. "No-one seems to be able to live in silence any more, though at least Jean-Philippe chooses quiet, soothing music."

"Very true. I do love my peaceful dog walks, just enjoying the sounds of the countryside. And the odd woof!" She laughed.

They had hardly begun their drinks when the main door burst open and in swept Feargal, his thin form draped in a loose, baggy shirt with the sleeves rolled up. He waved and shortly joined them with his coffee, and as usual, a massive sandwich.

"Well?" said Tamsin. "We're all agog! What have you learnt?"

Feargal took a big mouthful of his sandwich and waved his hand for them to wait while he chewed. At last he said, "Susannah. Found something about her history. Not in the archives, but by talking to one or two people. I found a bloke who'd been sweet on her a few years back. Learnt a lot!" He took another big mouthful. At this rate it wouldn't be long before the large sandwich was history.

Tamsin and Emerald both leaned forward attentively. "Go on!"

He finished chewing, took a swig of coffee, and said, "She hasn't been too lucky in love, it seems. Before this suitor met her, he says she'd been, let us say, the object of none-too-welcome attentions from a man here in Malvern. Once she found out he was married, she gave him the heave-ho. Seems he had been truly smitten, took it very bad and actually fled the country."

"And he was already married, you say?"

"Yep, left the wife too. Cleared out, lock, stock and barrel. Gone."

"So - who was this?"

"That's the pain. I'm still trying to find out. My informant only knew the story, not the name."

Tamsin sank back in her chair. "So all we've done is stirred up a bit of salacious gossip about Susannah."

"Sorry guys. You told me to sniff. And I sniffed!"

"Of course. I'm just disappointed. Think you'll be able to find out more? Doesn't seem likely, but there could be a link somehow ..."

"Feargal is on the case! Seriously, I'll keep going. We have precious little else. I'm working through the names you gave me who attended Mabel's ill-fated tea party. I'll keep looking at them too - see if there's any connection. So far *niente*."

Just then the door opened and several of Emerald's 6 o'clock students came in together, all sporting bags for their yoga mats and towels, heading for the welcoming smile of Kylie behind the counter.

"This is your lot of eager yogis, right?" Feargal asked of Emerald. "I'd better leave you to it. Bye!" and snatching up the last morsel of sandwich and with a whoosh of his baggy shirt he was up and out of the café.

"*Toujours pressé*," said a deep voice as Jean-Philippe arrived at their table, looking over his shoulder at the departing journalist. And seeing Emerald's puzzled expression, he added, "Always in a hurry, him."

"Oh yes, Feargal doesn't let the grass grow!" Tamsin smiled.

"And is the grass growing in your case? Or do you have some answers?"

"We have *some* answers, Jean-Philippe. I don't think you'll have to worry about keeping your baked goods under lock and key any more."

"Oh, *c'est merveilleux!* You have caught *le méchant?*"

"Let's say we've nailed him. And warned him off," Tamsin folded her arms in front of her. "And look who's coming over to join us .. better change the subject to more uplifting things, I think."

Jean-Philippe gave a handsome gallic bow as he pulled over some more chairs for the yoga students, now precariously carrying trays of drinks as well as their yoga bags.

Emerald made space at the table, keen to welcome her students. As several of them also knew Tamsin through taking their dogs to her classes too, they settled down to chat straight away.

"Tamsin!" said a child's voice.

"Hi Cameron, how're you doing? Taught Buster any new tricks?"

"We're doing Roll Over. He's ever so good at it."

"He has a good teacher," smiled Tamsin as the nine-year-old, looking important, turned his attention to his chocolate doughnut.

"Once you gave him your secret method he did it really fast!" said Molly. "I expect Alex and Joe are doing it even now. They think it's such fun." She looked at her intently. "You really made a difference with our family pet, Tamsin. When I see how some people have such trouble with their dogs, I'm really glad we found you when we did."

"I'm glad too, Molly. Your family is a source of endless entertainment for me!"

"Are you finding the *murderer?*" Cameron had polished off his doughnut and was wanting another diversion. Molly raised her eyes heavenward, but knew that Tamsin enjoyed chatting with her eldest son.

"Not exactly. We've got some clues. But haven't pieced them together yet. What do *you* think, Cameron?"

"I think ... maybe she was a bossy old woman and someone got fed up with her bossiness." He looked eagerly at Tamsin to see how she received his idea. "Then they climbed up a drainpipe and .. and .." he raised his arm and chopped it down dramatically, "killed her!"

"You could be right, young detective! That's highly possible for a motive. Not sure about the drainpipe, though. Trouble is, we don't have any evidence." Cameron frowned and drew on the straw of his fizzy drink while he thought.

A chair was drawn up beside Tamsin, and Shirley squashed herself into it. "Tamsin! I saw the ruckus at the market on Saturday! You're amazing. I never saw that creep move so fast."

"You know him?"

"Not at all. But if anyone can recognise a wrong'un by now, it's me," she said, her chins wobbling. "At least this is one that hasn't inveigled my son into trouble."

"How's Mark doing? Still at the bike shop?"

"Yes, and he's staying there, touch wood," and she gripped the edge of the mahogany table. "He's doing well. He'll have his mechanic qualification soon." And she allowed herself a smug smile.

"That's wonderful news! Do send him my best wishes," said Tamsin admiringly, thinking of all the probations and jail sentences Shirley had had to navigate with her errant son. "How's Luke managing in this weather?"

"Pyrenean Mountain Dogs do quite well in the heat, surprisingly. His white coat is so thick, it keeps a lot of the heat out. Like sheep, I suppose. But he does like to lie out flat on the verandah, in the shade. But tell me, Tamsin," Shirley shifted in her seat and stared at Tamsin, "what did your dog actually do to that man?"

"John Curtin? Banjo didn't do anything *to* him. He just sniffed around him and identified a scent I was looking for."

"What's this?" another voice chimed in. This time it was Saffron. "What were you doing?"

"Oh, hi Saffron. A bit of scentwork. Banjo is training in Search & Rescue, so we take every opportunity to sniff things out."

"Like owner, like dog!" chortled Saffron as she rummaged in her yoga bag. "You're always sniffing things out, Tamsin - oh no!" And she pulled out a rather scruffy, much-loved, soft toy. "It's Fuzzy Bear! Napoleon must have dropped it in my bag. I'll have to ring the babysitter - Charlie will never sleep without it. Excuse me .." And the harassed mother withdrew and started tapping away at her phone.

"Some things never change," smiled Shirley with amusement. "But I hear she's working part-time at that health shop of Linda's?"

"So I believe. She's recovering well from all the hoo-hah. Moving on. Good luck to her and her little boy!"

"I've got it!" cried Cameron. "It was the postman. He got so fed up climbing up all those steps to the lady's house that he decided to end it all."

"Come on, Sherlock!" laughed his mother, gathering up their bags.

It was time to start the class, and Emerald rose and shepherded her charges towards the stairs to the upper room at the back of the café. They shouldered their bags and wove their way through the tables, Saffron managing to bat a customer over the head with Fuzzy Bear as she wriggled past a chair. "So sorry, so sorry!" she chattered, as they all disappeared up the stairs, leaving a vacuum in the café.

Tamsin was staring into space when she became aware of Jean-Philippe collecting up all the crocks. "Here you go," she passed her own mug over to him. "Heard anything of interest lately?"

"Not much, I'm afraid. I see the *Mercury's* campaign is still active." He nodded towards a newspaper lying on the next table. "But you say the contaminations are *finis?*"

"I sincerely hope so. Assuming it was all being done by the one person. Doesn't get us any nearer to the murderer, though," she sighed.

"Still think they're connected?" Jean-Philippe put the last two mugs on his tray and started wiping the tables with his ever-present tea-towel.

"I think that the murderer took advantage of the tainting. I don't think they are otherwise connected." She leaned forward, causing the barista to do the same so their heads were almost touching. "There's been another attempted murder. We're not out of the woods yet."

Jean-Philippe straightened up again, shaking his head. *"Bon Dieu!* Is there no end to this?"

"The police are well and truly involved now. But we have something they don't - we have ears and move about the town and the Hills watching. And listening. Do tell me anything you find out, won't you Jean-Philippe?"

"Mais naturellement!" he replied, his thick black eyebrows travelling up his forehead in two big arches. "And right now there is something I can tell you .."

"Yes?" she sat up straighter.

"Oui, here is your friend, Madame Charity!"

Tamsin smiled with pleasure as the old lady spotted her, let go of the lead, and Muffin ran across to greet her. It wasn't long before the friends were sitting down together, Muffin on her owner's lap as usual, a fresh cup of tea and mug of coffee before them.

CHAPTER TWENTY-SEVEN

It was pleasantly cool in the café, and Charity's rosy cheeks were evidence that it was still hot outside. "It's actually cool enough in here for Muffin to lie beside me on the chair. That's so welcome in the winter, but I can't do it at home at the moment." She fanned her face with her hand as she gazed dotingly at her small fluffy brown dog.

"Mine can't understand why I don't want them on my lap too! And Opal absolutely doesn't get it. But this weather won't go on for ever."

"Three weeks of high temperatures! Almost unheard of these days. Though I can remember as a girl the summer days were hot and sunny, with thunderstorms every night!"

"I think it's possible that that story has grown somewhat in the telling, Charity!" Tamsin laughed.

"We do like to look back through rose-tinted spectacles, it's true." Charity's mouth turned down at the corners for a moment. "And I did have a happy childhood. Simple. Poor. But content. We didn't race around all the time back in those days. A bicycle was the fastest thing we normally encountered in Nether Trotley. And life went on from day to day …"

Tamsin' snapped her fingers. "Come back, Charity! They say this weather's going to break before much longer. Some people are loving it. But I'll be happy to get back to normal temperatures."

"It's nice to see so many children nut-brown and healthy from being outside. They often look so pale and washed-out from sitting in front of screens all day."

"There I'd have to agree with you. Now," Tamsin drank some of her coffee, "what's the latest, Charity?"

"Well, dear. I hear that you've been stirring things up in the market. Hilda said there was quite a scene on Saturday." She raised an eyebrow enquiringly, waiting to be filled in with the gory details.

"You know Hilda? Of course you do. Silly me." Tamsin smiled. "Yes, we collared the pest who's been trying to ruin the artisan makers. Caught him red-handed. Or 'scent-handed'. Banjo sniffed him out. Found he was reeking of the bitter stuff that he's been putting in the produce. Bloke called John Curtin."

Charity clapped her hands like a small child, causing Muffin to look up and make a muffled bark. "Clever Banjo! And clever you, my dear, to be able to do all that kind of thing. I'm so impressed." She looked sadly at Muffin for a moment.

"I know what you're thinking, Charity. But Muffin could learn that just as well."

"You really think so?"

"Absolutely. I saw her burrowing under your armchair once to reach the tiniest morsel of biscuit that she couldn't possibly have seen."

"I suppose you're right. You'll have to teach us at your Trotley class!"

"Done. I'll design something for the next round of classes. Chas and Cameron will be there with Buster, and they're dying to teach him some new tricks."

"Oh, that's nice! Such a lovely family. The children are so well-mannered."

"They are indeed. Anyway, I hope Hilda won't have to worry about her scones any more. I made it clear to Curtin that I'd be telling the police if there was any more of his nastiness."

"That's so good to hear. I'll tell her! And really, there's no need to be cluttering up prisons with the likes of that man, if he can be stopped with a warning."

"So that's what I've been doing. How about you? Any thoughts on Mabel's murder?"

"I can't think of anything new. I still think she was wholly innocent and it was a rehearsal. Just a feeling I have."

"I remember you saying that. Horrific. Such a callous disregard for life. But it seems you may be right."

"No!" gasped Charity.

"Yep. You know - of course you know - Susannah, the goatkeeper?"

"Lovely girl, yes indeed. I knew her grandmother. She chased after a boy I had my eye on."

"Did she get him?"

"I'm afraid she did. He would be Susannah's grandfather. So what's up with dear Susannah?"

"It seems someone tried to poison her."

Charity's eyes opened wide, as did her mouth.

"But don't worry, Charity, she's fine. She's absolutely fine. Fortunately Emerald and I were with her when she was about to take the poison, and my instinct made me stop her."

"Oh, but that's appalling. Where was this poison? I mean, how did she come to nearly take it? Some veterinary potion for her goats?"

"No, it was in some chocolates she'd been sent for appraisal. It was the exact same poison that killed Mabel Carstairs - very difficult to get hold of."

"Then can't you do the same thing you did for the man with the bitter-tasting stuff? Set Banjo to identify the murderer?"

"No way, Charity! I'm not letting my dogs near a lunatic with a phial of poison! They're far too precious."

"Of course! You're right." Charity tutted. "If this criminal can murder *people*, they'd have no qualms about 'just a dog'!" Charity laid a protective hand on Muffin's back, whose nose twitched in her sleep as her tail gave one flip.

"Oh, thank goodness you and Emerald were there to protect Susannah. Really, it doesn't bear thinking about."

"Sadly we have to think about it." Tamsin reached for her coffee mug, found it empty, and returned it to the table. "I seem to have spent the afternoon drinking coffee," she grinned, as she drank some water instead. "Probably time to stop. We don't have any idea why Susannah was targeted. Whether it's personal, or she's the final intended victim. Thallium is a slow-acting poison. So presumably if she had eaten a chocolate or two she'd have started showing symptoms, then they'd have to have another go with more of the stuff to actually kill her."

"So that means Mabel was poisoned over a period too."

"That's why we first thought of her nephew and her carer. Both seem highly unlikely. Feargal's checking over the guests Mabel had in her home a week or so before. It was a sort of stand-around buffet event, so they could easily have got at something she ate regularly."

"Like her corn flakes?"

"Something like that," Tamsin smiled.

"I hope that nice young man who makes cider wasn't at that party?"

"Charity! You're a witch! I won't even ask you what you're thinking," laughed Tamsin as Charity pursed her lips and feigned innocence, then she said, "So supposing Mabel wasn't a rehearsal and Susannah is the intended victim this time, does that mean we have another madman loose?"

"I don't think that's possible. Thallium is hard to get here in England."

"Where does it come from?"

"It's used - legally - in lens manufacture. That's why I thought of Reggie first of all. He's something to do with top secret laser beam work which involves specialist lenses. But apart from the fact that I really don't think it was him, the police will have interviewed him thoroughly. He must be in the clear."

"Ok. Where else can it be found?"

"It's used in plenty of scientific processes. So presumably it's readily available at the Science Park. That's why I was wondering if John Curtin was the murderer." She sighed. "But I really think he isn't. He's too weaselly - just vindictive."

"Is that it? It's only available to scientists?"

"Um," Tamsin thought hard. "Oh yes, there's one other place. They use it in the Middle East to kill vermin. It's easy to get there apparently .." She stopped dead, her eyes staring into the middle distance, her hands clutching the table. "The Middle East!" She jumped to her feet. "Charity, you've done it again. I have to go!" And so saying she raced out into the still hot street, and jogged back across the Common to her home.

CHAPTER TWENTY-EIGHT

By the time she arrived home she needed a shower, but first buzzed a text off to Feargal. Getting dressed again in something loose and cool, but still wearing her shorts with their - to the dogs - all-important pockets, one of which always contained treats, she drank two glasses of water before heading out with her flock to the shade of the ash tree.

It wasn't long before Feargal rang her back. "What's up, kiddo?"

"Bless you, Feargal!" she smirked at his greeting, although Feargal couldn't see that. "I've just realised something. I mean I knew it already - I just hadn't registered it properly: too stupid! I was so busy thinking the source of the thallium had a science connection that I completely forgot that it's readily available in the Middle East. And who worked in the Middle East fairly recently?"

"Dolores?"

"You knew?"

"I'm guessing. I'm putting two and two together. I've found out the identity of the man who was besotted with Susannah, and then bolted."

"No!"

"Yes. His name was Ernest Baxter. Dolores was his wife."

"Oh-oh-oh. It's all falling into place ... Dolores was chewed up with rejection and loss, and tried to get her own back on the only person she could reach."

"The person she thought was at the bottom of her troubles. Remember, Ernest Baxter picked her up in Spain, where she was born, and whisked her off to rainy England. She gave up everything for him."

"And he deceived her. I can quite see that would make any woman angry. But she's blaming the wrong person."

"Rationality doesn't get much of a look-in when someone is seething with hatred."

"I think we should go round there. At least stop her doing anything more to Susannah."

"I'll see you there in fifteen minutes. Park round the corner."

"Right you are." And Tamsin chewed her lip pensively as she finished the call. "I suppose we'll have to tell Hawkins," she confided to the dogs, who didn't even flick an ear, so flat out asleep they all were. "But I'd like to talk to her first. Very sad." She heard a miaow from the back doorway, and found she did have an audience after all. "Ok, ok, Opal. In the absence of your primary feeder I'll come and fill your bowl." And she chuckled as she went back into the house, followed by a procession of quadrupeds.

She was sitting in her car in the next road to Dolores's house when Feargal appeared. As he put his hand on the door handle she released the lock and he hopped in.

"I have a photocopy of the note from the chocolates parcel," he said tersely.

Tamsin gaped at him. "Your mole got you that?"

"Mm-hm." He raised an eyebrow.

"She must be crazy about you."

"Who said it's a 'she'?" he grinned.

Tamsin shook her head in wonderment. "Ok, that will probably be useful. Dolores must have typed it on her own typewriter, or more likely at the house of one of her clients. The police will find that out easily enough. Let's go."

They walked to Dolores's house and knocked on the door. All was quiet.

"Hello cat," said Feargal, as one of Dolores's cats wound itself round his leg.

"Her cat," said Tamsin, as the other one sat watching them from an upturned bucket, mewing plaintively. "Why are they shut out? I don't remember seeing a cat-flap."

"Let's go round the back."

And when they reached the back door they saw that the kitchen window was open. Feargal tried the door and it opened. Knocking loudly, he called out "Dolores? Mrs. Baxter?" as the cats came in past him and sat expectantly on the kitchen table.

On Feargal's nod, Tamsin quietly climbed the stairs, knocking on each door before opening it. Feargal checked the downstairs rooms.

"Mess everywhere," he said as she came down the stairs again, and Tamsin, shaking her head, said, "Worse upstairs. Bed unmade, clothes scattered about. She's done a flit."

They went back to the kitchen.

"Hey, what's this?" Tamsin saw the corner of a sheet of paper sticking out from under one of the cats. She shifted his tail and picked up the sheet, which she and Feargal read together.

"So she knew we were on to her."

Feargal pointed to the second line. "This bit about seeing Susannah fit and well in Malvern this morning. Seems to have shown her the game was up."

"Yeah, if she'd eaten any of those chocolates she should have been pretty ill already."

"Look, there's a load more on the back!"

Tamsin snatched the sheet and read it out loud, skipping over the spelling mistakes and correcting the broken English as she read."Susannah ruined my life. Ernest and I were happy. We had a beautiful house, and it made up for missing the sun of my home country. Then he met that cow. She must have encouraged him. She led him on. Then she rejected him. It affected his mind. He left for somewhere in Europe, I don't know where. He took his money and left me with nothing. I had to sell the house and live in this hole. I went to the Middle East for some heat and to earn some easy money. Except it wasn't easy. It was like slavery. But they are very free with their poisons over there.'" She flapped the paper over again. "It doesn't say where she's going."

"She can't have been planning to top herself - no need to pack for that."

"And she left the window open so someone would find the cats ... I wonder ..." Tamsin gazed at the picture on the wall - the sun dancing on the blue of the sea, the gaily-coloured umbrellas shading the little tables. She turned to Feargal, "She's gone home."

"She can't have gone long. There's still time to catch her!" And he whipped out his phone and got through to Chief Inspector Hawkins' office. "Would you tell the Chief that his murderer is on her way to Spain? You'll need to issue an All Ports warning." He peered at the picture, which had the name of the town in the bottom corner, and filled in all the details for the astonished constable tapping out notes at the other end of the phone. "There's a note here. You'll be sending someone round to look over the house and collect it?"

"Straight away. Your name, sir?"

"Oh, Hawkins will enjoy guessing that," he grinned, and cut off the call.

"Poor Dolores. She's been festering all these years. Forced to live in this grotty house, doing menial tasks for others - some of them with big, grand houses. She got bitter."

"And twisted. Yes. Poor woman. But she has to be caught. One murder, one attempted murder."

"Perhaps Mabel annoyed her one day. After all, she didn't seem to be that disabled. She probably used Dolores more as a skivvy."

"Stop siding with her! She killed someone!"

"She did. And - almost worse in my eyes - she abandoned her cats! I'll call the shelter right now."

CHAPTER TWENTY-NINE

"So," said Tamsin putting down her coffee mug and leaning back in The Cake Stop's most comfortable armchair, "they caught her at Birmingham International Airport. Apparently she broke down completely, sobbing and screaming."

Charity tutted and shook her head slowly.

Susannah twisted her hands in her lap and asked, "What will happen to her now?"

Feargal spoke kindly, "She's safely locked up, awaiting psychiatric reports before trial. She's made a full confession."

Susannah shuddered again and Emerald put a hand on her shoulder.

Charity turned to her and said quietly, "So how did you get caught up in this, dear?"

"It came back to me later, after Tamsin asked if I knew a Dolores. I said I didn't. But you see, there was a man .."

"It's always a man," said Emerald.

"When will we ever learn?" smiled Tamsin. "Go on, do."

"Well, this man - I thought him quite attractive. It was before I started the goat farm. I was working in the Library in Malvern - it was a while ago. He was always coming in and looking at travel books. But he kind of hit on me. And wouldn't leave me alone. To start with I liked him, but then I found out he was married, so I told him to shove it. He became more and more difficult. I was on the point of calling on the police to help. But then he upped sticks and left - I've no idea where he went, but one of the others at the library had heard he'd gone. He left me, his job, his wife ..."

"Dolores?" asked Emerald quietly.

"His name was Ernest Baxter. Dolores was his wife."

They were all quiet for a moment. "But it wasn't your fault!" protested Emerald. "Why did she blame you?"

"Commonsense kinda goes out the window when people are suffering," said Feargal.

Charity spoke out, "They have to blame someone. It's easier to be angry with someone else than to manage the grief."

"Of course, Charity - you're right. It's all very sad," agreed Tamsin. "And as for that idiot Curtin! I think his actions inspired Dolores to do something. She thought she could work under cover of his contaminations. The police have spoken to him, by the way. They decided he was no longer a danger and not worth wasting public money on. But they've warned him off good-o!"

"He has to be on his best behaviour from now on. They've marked his card," said Feargal.

"And he may forget all about applying to the Craft Market! Felicity has blocked him. The individuals affected could sue him privately of course."

"But we're English and we don't tend to bother with that sort of thing!" Feargal chuckled.

"Probably a huge waste of time and emotion. Best to move on, I would think," Charity nodded wisely, her lips pursed.

"I wonder if he'll get the message and move away from the area?" wondered Emerald.

"That would be a very good idea, all round!"

"Ah, *Mesdames et Monsieur!*" a familiar deep voice interrupted them. "The Furies are fully *occupées* baking today. But Damaris brought over this special edition of their hazelnut meringue this morning," and he presented a splendid creamy meringue concoction, with a large white sugar goat perched unsteadily on the top.

Tamsin clapped her hands in childlike pleasure, and Kylie set to, making space on the table for the cake and plates and forks.

"Penelope wanted you to have this as a token of their gratitude," Jean-Philippe continued, his large black eyebrows knitting together as he remembered the words exactly, "She said, 'For all you have done for the creative people in Malvern, Thank you Tamsin!' *Voilà!*" He nodded to Kylie who began cutting the cake.

The mood lifted as they enjoyed the sumptuous meringue, Tamsin managing to drop blobs of cream on her shorts. She put a fingerful in her mouth and said, "This cream is so white!"

Susannah smiled. "Electra ordered three pots of goats' cream for this morning. I had no idea what the Furies were up to!" and she reached out to touch the sugar goat. "This is wonderful!"

"You must have it!" said Emerald. "We'll get something to wrap it in for you to take home."

"But I think you may need to keep it in the fridge till this weather breaks!" smiled Charity, who was surreptitiously giving her finger to Muffin to lick.

And it was a good while later when, replete, they all left the cool coffee shop and made their several ways home. By the time Tamsin and Emerald had walked across the crunchy brown grass on the Common they were both complaining about the sultry heat.

"It's so close - I'm dripping!" said Tamsin. "Bagsy the shower first." She looked at Emerald as they approached the house, "I don't know how you always look so cool and ethereal!"

They went in and withstood the rapturous greeting from Quiz, Banjo, and Moonbeam, who had been sleeping peacefully and were delighted their people were home again.

Opal padded quietly across the floor and gazed hopefully at her food-bowl.

"No chance!" said Emerald. "You'll have to wait till ..." and she was interrupted by a crack of thunder, so loud that Banjo started barking.

And a sound they hadn't heard for weeks completely captivated them - starting slowly then gathering speed, the drumming of rain on the sunroom roof!

They all ran out to the little garden and danced in the wonderful healing rain, the dogs rolling about on the wet grass in their joy, Tamsin and Emerald laughing merrily, while Opal gazed in wonder at this madness from the safety of the dry doorway.

Ready for Snapped and Framed! *- the next book in this popular series? You'll find it here:*

https://mybook.to/SnappedFramed

And this time, Tamsin will be doing her detecting with the aid of a camera, when one of the new photography class students is found dead on Midsummer Hill! Can Tamsin's brave dogs save a lost child as well as capturing the crook? Read it now ...

^^^ Scan the code above or click here

To find out how Tamsin arrived in Malvern and began Top Dogs, you can read this free novella "Where it all began" at

https://urlgeni.us/Lucyemblemcozy

and we'll be able to let you know when Tamsin's next adventure is ready for you!

And if you enjoyed this book, I'd love it if you could whiz over to where you bought it and leave a brief review, so others may find it and enjoy it as well, and be kind to their animals!

ABOUT THE AUTHOR

From an early age I loved animals. From doing "showjumping" in the back garden with Simon, the long-suffering family pet - many years before Dog Agility was invented - I worked in the creative arts till I came back to my first love and qualified as a dog trainer.

Working for years with thousands of dogs and their colourful owners - from every walk of life - I found that their fancies and foibles, their doings and their undoings, served to inspire this series of cozy mysteries.

While the varying characters weave their way through the books, some becoming established personnel in the stories, the stars of the show are the animals!

They don't have human powers. They don't need to. They have plenty of powers of their own, which need only patience and kindness to bring out and enjoy with them.

If you enjoyed this story, I would LOVE it if you could hop over to where you purchased your book and leave a brief review!

Lucy Emblem

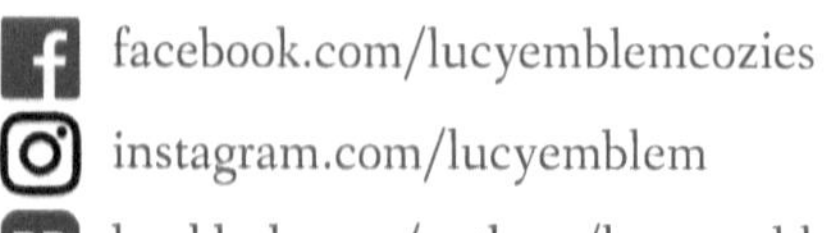

facebook.com/lucyemblemcozies
instagram.com/lucyemblem
bookbub.com/authors/lucy-emblem

ALL THE TAMSIN KERNICK COZY ENGLISH MYSTERIES

Where it all began ..

https://urlgeni.us/Lucyemblemcozy

Sit, Stay, Murder!

https://mybook.to/SitStayMurder

Ready, Aim, Woof!

https://mybook.to/ReadyAimWoof

Down Dog!

https://mybook.to/downdog

Barks, Bikes, and Bodies!

https://mybook.to/BarksBikesBodies

Ma-ah, Ma-ah, Murder!

https://mybook.to/TamsinKernickCozies

Snapped and Framed!

https://mybook.to/SnappedFramed

Also available in Large Print

https://mybook.to/TamsinKernickCozies